*To my granddaughter, "Katy" Katelyn Elizabeth Synder,
whose name I have borrowed for this book;*

*and to Elizabeth "Lizzie" Wiggin Ridlon,
whose brother—my great-grandfather, George Wiggin—
served in Co. B, 29th Regiment,
Maine Infantry of the Union Army;*

*and to Jimmy Ridlon,
son of Elizabeth W. Ridlon,
who though his memory is but a shadow in my mind,
also lent his name to this book about Maine people
of his generation.*

Contents

Chapter 1

The Elms

Maggie Ridlon's long, red ringlets flew and sparkled in the slanting rays of the afternoon late-summer sun as she flipped over lightly on the flat, granite boulder at the water's edge and hitched the folds of her green calico skirt beneath her slender legs. "My freckles have had quite enough sun for today," Maggie told herself decidedly, lying on her stomach and pushing the bill of a faded blue Civil War soldier's cap from her forehead to peer out across the lake. Her cap had belonged to her father, Sergeant Major James Ridlon, whose name she shared. He was shot while leading his unit of Yankee soldiers along Little Round Top during the Battle of Gettysburg, weeks before she, Margaret James Ridlon, was born in 1863.

The Elms, the Maine woods horse farm where Maggie, though barely twelve, had chosen to make her home with Grandpa Bill Fuller, spread its green acres along Allagash Lake's rocky shores. The Elms' tall white house and long, gray-shingled barn now cast their growing shadows across the landscape.

Maggie propped herself on her elbows, cushioned in a pocket of the huge, mossy rock, and gazed across the water. Satisfied that the men towing a raft of logs with the North Woods Logging Company's side-wheeled steam tugboat were too far away to notice her unladylike behavior, she kicked her bare feet up to the late August sun and let her skirt slide to her knees. A nip had hung in the air most of the day, and it felt good to have the warmth of these rays that would soon give way to fall's sharp chills.

"Winter's comin', ol' Bowse," remarked Maggie affectionately, hugging Bowser, who had found his own spot on the boulder. Her half-beagle hound, colored mostly white with a saddle of brown on his back, seemed unconcerned. The grass had been silvered with frost that morning, and Grandpa had mentioned that he'd soon need to pick his garden pumpkins and cut the last of his corn to feed Molly, their one Jersey cow. But Bowser had full assurance that, whatever the weather, his mistress would meet his needs.

"Who cares about winter, anyway, eh?" Maggie said at last. She sat up and, dangling her legs into the water, drew Bowser's head onto her lap as she stroked the coarse, short hairs of his white neck.

Bowser only rolled his languid brown eyes upward. Maggie kissed his wet nose. "Jacky doesn't love you, but *I* love you dearly," she pouted, half in anger, half in jest. "So it's just you 'n' me 'n' Grandpa this winter!"

By now, the tug had towed the logs out of sight into the lake's outlet stream toward the distant sawmill on Chamberlain Lake, and the fading "chuff-chug, chuff-chug" of its steam engine told Maggie that the boat was now well off in the distance. The crew, she knew, would not return for more logs this late in the afternoon. Too, she could hear the faint "thud, thud, thud" of Grandpa's hammer as he repaired a stall in the great old horse stable beyond the house. So, satisfied that she was alone, Maggie tossed her blouse and skirt and her soldier's cap off onto the rock, and tying her ankle-length petticoat around her waist, she splashed in her frilly bloomers toward a sandbar she could see under the shadowy water just a few dozen feet from shore.

Though the water was icy, it was shallow at first, so Maggie pushed on until she reached a sunken log. Between her and the sandbar now lay a deep pool. Maggie spread her toes and bent one knee, feeling for the lake bottom. By now her bloomers were wet, but, little concerned, she had adjusted to the frigid cold of the late-summer lake.

She tried the bottom; it was mud, shin deep. Too late! Suddenly, her other foot slipped from the submerged log, and Maggie was in over her head.

Learning to swim was not a privilege afforded girls growing up in New England right after the Civil War. Laketon, Maine, where her mother's neat, white clapboard cottage nestled on a narrow side street, was at the foot of vast Moosehead Lake. But each afternoon all summer, a troop of noisy boys would romp down their picket-lined lane, then cross the peninsula east of the village to engage in the exclusively masculine recreation of swimming.

Maggie had once seen a photo of female bathers at Atlantic City in *Harper's Weekly*. They were dressed sillily, she thought, in bloomers and knee-length dresses. Soaking wet, they reminded her of Mother's hens after a sudden summer rain!

Fortunately for Maggie, she had fallen in the direction of the submerged sandbar, and she quickly scrambled up, clawing underwater with her toes as she held her breath. Pawing the water, she fought to keep her feet beneath her in chest-deep water. She was now stranded in the lake, but her head and shoulders were out, at least.

Bowser, who had thought his mistress was simply enjoying a merry splash, paddled happily alongside. She took a deep breath and made a frantic decision. Wrapping one arm around the paddling dog, Maggie kicked off from the sandbar toward shore.

It was a quarter to five by the time wet dog and sodden girl sloshed into the kitchen of the old, high-ceilinged farmhouse that Maggie shared with her grandfather and dog. The fire in the cast-iron Queen Atlantic kitchen range had burned down to embers, but the stove was still warm, she discovered. As she leaned over, shivering, her wet hair dripped onto the stove lids, the drops sizzling on the hot cast-iron cooking surface, sending a cloud of warm moisture to her grateful face.

Finally, Maggie checked the apple pies she had left in the oven before going to sun herself on the rock. To her relief, they were done nicely and were not at all burnt. She slammed the oven door shut, and the mantel clock began to strike five, jarred into its melodious activity several seconds ahead of schedule by the door's dull thud.

An ominous scrape of heavy boots on the mat in the long shed leading from the house to the horse stables caught Maggie's ear. Grandpa was tending the logging company's horses, and he would soon want his supper, she realized, as his arthritic, shuffling tread moved closer. She fled into the hall toward the stairs to her bedroom as Grandpa Fuller opened the kitchen door.

❦ ❦ ❦

Maggie cried herself to sleep that night, with only flop-eared Bowser curled against her knees to offer slight comfort. In the two weeks since she had trekked with Grandpa by canoe, logging train, and portage from her childhood home in Laketon, journeying the sixty miles north to the wilderness horse farm, Maggie had not until today stopped to consider the life changes that, young as she was, she now faced.

Maggie's mother, Katherine Fuller, widowed since shortly before Maggie was born, had married John Hanscombe in June. During Mama's two-week honeymoon, Maggie had been left with Grandmother Ridlon, a tired old lady with little patience with girls. Grandmother Ridlon had herself been widowed young. After her only child—Maggie's father, Jimmy Ridlon—had lost his life to a Confederate musket ball outside Gettysburg in 1863, the elder Mrs. Ridlon, bereaved of her son, had only reluctantly opened her home to occasional visits from her half-orphaned granddaughter.

Then Mama Katy and Stepfather John had come home from their honeymoon at the seacoast. With them came Jacky Hanscombe, John's son, just a few months older than Maggie. Jacky had been staying with his grandmother in Augusta. A city boy, he soon let it be known that he found small village folks rather rude and rustic—"quaint," he said of Laketon's small-town manners, quoting his citified grandmother.

Right away Jacky let Maggie know for certain that he had no use for a country dog like Bowser, who was little more than a pup. He'd once shoved "that mangy mongrel" out of his room, slamming the door on the hapless hound's tender tail. Then, when Jacky beat Bowser for carrying off and chewing up his collection of gray and red squirrel tails that he'd carelessly left on a sitting room chair, Maggie decided something must be done.

She would move out.

Two years ago, when Grandma Lucy Fuller died, Maggie had spent a month at The Elms with Grandpa, here on Allagash Lake, helping him keep house while he kept the horses for the North Woods Logging Company. Now she would become his housekeeper permanently, Maggie had told herself.

The Elms, Maggie had first thought, was about as near heaven as one could get without actually being there. The house, a grand mansion of Colonial design, had been built nearly half a century earlier as the summer residence of the North Woods' company president. It had two tall chimneys, but the massive fireplaces in every room had years earlier been closed up with brick and plaster and replaced with wood-burning stoves.

A long ell, which housed a woodshed and Grandpa's workshop, ran behind the house, clear to a cavernous, heavy-beamed, gray-shingled barn at the far end, connecting house and barn in northcountry New England fashion so that the farmer need not go outside to do his chores in foul weather. Four dozen teams of Percheron workhorses were housed in this long barn several months a year. The barn's spacious loft held winter hay not only for these horses, but for the company's other sturdy, heavy-hoofed beasts that drew great loads of logs from the forest on wagons or pungs.

In winter, the horses, except for mares in foal, were kept in drafty temporary paddocks at the logging camps. And Grandpa Fuller had told Maggie that much of The Elms' supply of hay was taken from the barn to feed the horses in the deep woods. In winter, the lakes and broader forest rivers and streams became smooth, frozen forest roads over which men could drive teams of trotting, steel-shod horses pulling loads of hay to the logging camps along the way.

Behind the farmstead, The Elms' broad acres stretched, green with grass and clover, to the endless forests of spruce and pine beyond. Gray, mossy stone walls with weathered cedar rails on top partitioned the fields, which in midsummer were sprinkled with yellow buttercups, white daisies, and black-eyed Susans.

Elm trees, rising in goblet-shaped profiles, stood wherever fence joined fence. Here nestled the lonesome little world that Maggie had recently chosen as her own. Here, except for an occasional woodsman or a hunter, from time to time the tugboat crew, or the men of the haying crew who came in July, she, Grandpa, and Bowser lived in their big house, its barn with the horses, one milking Jersey, a cat, six laying hens, and a speckled Sussex rooster to herald the dawn.

But Maggie's forest family was not entirely alone, for she had often seen the white-tailed deer that came to graze in the fields at dusk. One evening from her bedroom window, she had counted more than thirty, led by a grave old buck, his wary nostrils drinking the night air for human scent, his summer antlers still lush with velvet.

Squirrels by the dozen, both gray and red, chattered their complaints from the oaks that lined the lake. White-waistcoated swallows sailed after garden insects from May to September from their nests under the barn's eaves. And speckled bobwhites whistled all the month of August from the raspberry thickets in the fence corners. Blue jays and black crows added their shrill cries from the elm trees along the stone walls behind the garden. And once, in the moonlight, Maggie had shivered in terrified delight as she watched a broad-winged great-horned owl capture a half-grown coon, caught robbing Grandpa's corn patch.

But tonight Maggie was miserable.

It was not the daily round of cooking and laundry and cleaning from dawn till dusk with only a brief break in the afternoon that made Maggie sad, for she had been an efficient housekeeper from the time she was a small girl. Nor was it the dunking in the icy Allagash Lake that had so suddenly and rudely ended her sunny solitude on the mossy boulder that upset her. Nor was it even the scolding she had gotten from Grandpa, when after toweling dry and changing her underclothes, she had come back downstairs to find him frying venison hash for their evening meal.

Though she had spent more than a month alone with Grandpa two years earlier, now after just two weeks, Maggie was homesick.

In a little over a week, Maggie remembered, the village school in Laketon would open for the fall session. Her desk, she considered with indignation, would not be empty, for her stepbrother, Jacky Hanscombe, would surely fill it. "And they won't even miss me," Maggie stewed to no one but Bowser, who only growled at an imaginary Indian in his sleep.

I'm so glad Mama married Stepfather John, but why did Jacky have to come when we were so happy? she pondered angrily. Life was changing faster than it had a right to, Maggie told herself as, alone in her room above the kitchen, she slipped off into a troubled sleep. She loved The Elms, but Maggie loved Mama even more. The terrible fact was that Maggie had chosen this bittersweet new life in anger.

Chapter 2

The Queen of the Manse

The deep "bong" of the tall grandfather clock on the front hall stairs landing stirred Maggie awake at last. She had heard the clock strike five, only seconds before, it seemed. Five-thirty came much too early. And now that it was almost autumn in the north woods, it was still dark when she had to rise and fix breakfast for herself and Grandpa.

Maggie slid her feet into her felt slippers and lit the kerosene lamp beside her bed. After giving her tangled locks a vigorous brushing with a mahogany-handled, boar-bristle brush, Maggie sleepily pulled an old blue army jacket over her flannel nightgown.

Maggie remembered Grandma Lucy Fuller whenever she used that hairbrush, for it had been hers. She smiled to herself when she recalled how, five years earlier visiting at The Elms with Mother, she had used this very brush to unsnarl the dirty tangles of Old Shep, Grandpa's aging collie, who since had gone to his reward.

The loneliness and sorrow that had plagued Maggie's sleep the evening before was forgotten for the moment in the excitement of a new day at The Elms. Much as Maggie loved Mother, she also did truly love The Elms and Grandpa. The freedom of her life here

16

with its rapidly expanding horizons excited and encouraged her each morning. Today she and Grandpa would begin a two-day canoe trip up Allagash Stream to visit lumber camps. Maggie had longed to see these places from the day she had arrived at Allagash Lake.

A thud of four frisky paws followed by the snapping of long hound ears reminded Maggie that she was not alone in her room. Bowser had sprung to life, so she seated herself on the bed again to watch his comical head shaking, clearing what Maggie imagined to be deep doggy cobwebs from his brain. His toenails click-clicked across the hard maple floor as he trotted to his mistress' side. Maggie scratched Bowser's head, then let him out the door.

She waited until Bowser rumbled down the back stairs and ripped through the leather-hung dog hole into the shed before turning back to her room. She loved this cozy little chamber above the kitchen. Grandpa had pointed out that it had been the maid's room in the days when the old mansion had been the residence of the sawmill company's president. He had even tried to talk her into taking as hers the room that once had been a grand bedroom for the president's daughter.

The daughter's former room was a large, airy boudoir at the far end of the main house, down the hall from where Grandpa slept in the upstairs master bedroom. But after one night in this room, with its ten-foot-high ceilings, tall windows, and high-posted canopy bed, Maggie had had quite enough. What seemed elegant and grand in the daylight she had found eerie in the dark. And the room was cold. The sun's warming rays never came to the north side of the house. Though Grandpa had promised that Maggie could have a fire in the room's small stove each evening, she had shook her head decidedly no.

So the maid's room had become hers. For years it had been used for storage, so Maggie was required to help Grandpa carry dozens of boxes and crates into the garret over the main house to get it ready. A register in the floor allowed warm air from the kitchen to heat the room.

Maggie's new room had all the enchantment of a secret chamber. She could take refuge in the back of the house with none but Bowser to disturb her. Yet through her cast-iron register in the floor she could spy into the kitchen on those below.

One evening Maggie had listened through the register as Grandpa and old Jacques "Jake" Beavertail had conversed for hours downstairs in the kitchen about trapping and hunting and fishing and logging. Jake sometimes broke into musical French when lost for *Anglais* words and phrases to express himself to Grandpa's English-tuned ears. Though Grandpa, she knew, understood little French and could speak less, Jake would enthusiastically demonstrate his words with his hands as Grandpa nodded and grinned at Jake's elaborate gestures.

Maggie's room was also unique in that it had a variety of entrances. The front entrance, which Maggie seldom used, was up three steps from the bedroom. It led through a heavy oaken door with brass hinges and marble knobs to the main upstairs hall lined with the bedrooms once occupied by the company president's family. Off this hall, also, was a bathroom with the only flush toilet Maggie had ever seen except for the time she had gone with Mama by train to Augusta, the state capital.

The bathroom had a tub, a huge wooden affair lined with sheets of soldered zinc. But, though The Elms' mansion was supplied with running water from the same elevated wooden tank and steel-framed windmill that watered the horses in the barn, Grandpa had flatly refused to consider letting Maggie take a tub bath. The hot water system hadn't worked for years, he pointed out. And since several of the tub's seams needed resoldering, and he had no plumber's forge or soldering iron, even carrying water upstairs from the kitchen was out of the question. Such a luxury "weren't worth the bother when there's plenty of hot water in the kitchen stove reservoir," Grandpa had declared.

So, like at home in Laketon, Maggie and Grandpa took turns sponging clean beside the hot kitchen stove each Saturday evening. It was important to take a bath on Saturday night, Maggie knew, for except for when she was living in the woods with Grandpa, she needed to be clean for church on Sunday.

And, as Grandpa had said, the copper reservoir built into the stove next to the oven always had plenty of water for a bath in the old wooden laundry tub. Unless one were wealthy, this was the way baths were taken all over the civilized world, as far as Maggie knew, so she never complained about not being able to use the leaky tub upstairs.

Maggie's favorite bedroom entrance, however, was the back one, through the simple pine door with its plain iron lift-latch. This door opened into a small landing and steep, narrow stairs that led down to the back entry, just outside the kitchen door. From this landing, too, Maggie could open a small door to a catwalk across the beams above the woodshed and on farther still over Grandpa's workshop. Picking her way across beams and loose planks, Maggie learned that she could travel all the way to the barn loft without going downstairs. She discovered a loose board where the ell joined the barn's wall, evidently left that way years ago to make a nocturnal passage for cats to roam, looking for mice in the haymow.

And behind mounds of loose hay, high from prying eyes far below, Maggie used a pitchfork and rake to fix herself a secret chamber, which she braced up with old boards she found under the barn. Into her hideout a shaft of light shone in the afternoon from a window high in the barn's south gable end, providing enough light to read her copies of *Great Expectations*, *Little Women*, and *Robinson Crusoe*.

Maggie's secret chamber was known only to her, Bowser, and Tabby, Grandpa's gray tiger tomcat.

The hall below Maggie's room was special, too, for it had five doors that took up most of its wall space. One door led into the kitchen and another to the cellar stairs, beneath her own back stairway. Still another led into the woodshed, and two others, one facing the front yard and the other facing the back, opened outdoors. Maggie's entrance, in fact, was the only one in the grand old house with outside doors front and rear. So Maggie alone had easy access to the entire mansion, the shed, and the barn from her room. Maggie, she told herself, was queen of the manse.

Her bedroom was even more special because it reminded her of her upstairs room in her home at Laketon. The slanted walls, papered in a pattern of mallard ducks among cattails and bulrushes, gave the room a cozy warmth, Maggie thought, as she stood that morning on the register above the kitchen stove, momentarily letting the heat from the fire beneath warm her legs under her flannel nightgown.

Fastening just two buttons of the old blue Civil War dress uniform coat that had been her father's, Maggie turned its long cuffs up to free her hands for work. She paused briefly by the mirror to adjust the coat's sleeves so that she could catch a glimpse of Father's sergeant major stripes. Lighting her way with the lamp, she hurried down to the kitchen, and last evening's feelings of homesickness began to return. "It's not fair," Maggie whispered to herself as she thought of the father she'd never known.

Across her imagination flitted the image of Sergeant Major James Ridlon, Co. B, 20th Regiment, Maine Infantry, as she reached for the kitchen door. Etched permanently on Maggie's mind was the tiny tintype figure of a soldier who peered from the oval ivory frame on her bedside table. He was a young man, thin and wiry, with a wispy beard that had scarcely begun to grow. The very coat she now wore across her shoulders was buttoned neatly across his hard chest as he stared fiercely at the camera.

Yet the image of Jim Ridlon that most often filled Maggie's mind was not of the young infantry sergeant trying to look tough for the camera. Rather, she remembered most vividly the stories Mother had told, and those few yellowed letters written in places like Antietam or Fredericksburg or Gettysburg, carefully stashed in Mother's bureau drawer. Though scarcely twenty years old, Jimmy Ridlon had been made a sergeant major. The last of these letters, written by one of his soldiers, had been wrapped up in Father's cap and coat and mailed to Mother. The letter told how Sergeant Major Ridlon had led twenty brave soldiers through cannon shot and musket fire until that day a musket ball had cut off his life.

John Hanscombe, on the other hand, had never been a soldier, Maggie reflected. Though his lack of military experience did not make him any less a man, Maggie grudgingly admitted to herself, it nonetheless in her eyes made Hanscombe less than her father, whom she secretly believed to be more than a mere man. Though, like Father, Hanscombe had volunteered for the Union Army, he was turned down because the doctors had suspected he had a tuberculosis infection, which since seemed to have disappeared.

Grandpa Fuller had likewise been a soldier and had followed General Sam Houston in pursuit of the Mexican tyrant Santa Anna across Texas, only days after the massacre of Davy Crockett, Jim Bowie, and the others at the Alamo. There had been Fullers and Ridlons in the Revolutionary War, too, Maggie knew. Family tradition held that some of her ancestors had fought the French and Indians in the Maine woods even before that.

But now as Maggie entered the kitchen these thoughts faded as she faced the tasks of the day. For the most part, Maggie found her tasks pleasant, even fun, for she was mistress of the house, queen of the mansion. She placed her lamp on the kitchen table, but its low flame only dimly lit the large country kitchen, with its long row of cupboards, its sink, butcher block, and cast-iron Queen Atlantic cooking range.

Maggie saw by the faint glow through the stove's grate that Grandpa had started a fire before taking his kerosene lantern and milk pail to the barn to do his morning chores. But she would need the stove hot enough to fry hash in the skillet, and the pine kindling he had left burning was nearly out. So, into the stove went five or six pieces of dry alder bush—"biscuit wood," Grandpa called it, because alders were ideal for a quick baking fire on a summer morning, yet they would burn themselves out before making the kitchen unbearably hot.

After putting a teakettle on the stove, Maggie turned her attention to the dumbwaiter, a small, hand-operated elevator built into a large kitchen cupboard, which she used as a refrigerator by lowering food into the cool cellar.

She turned the crank until a shelf appeared with a slab of smoked venison and a piece of deer suet. Maggie cut off enough to make breakfast hash. Returning the rest of the meat and suet to the dumbwaiter, she cranked them down to the cellar.

Maggie would need to have her skillet hot by the time Grandpa came in from the barn so she could have breakfast ready before he finished shaving. She lifted the large, black frying pan from its hook under the mantel behind the stove. Grandpa called this skillet a "spider." The long spider-like iron legs, now filed off, had once enabled a colonial housewife to fry her family's breakfast over a bed of coals in the fireplace. Maggie was happy that she, a modern housekeeper, had a fine iron stove with a polished top on which to cook meals for her and Grandpa.

A whining and a scratching at the kitchen door caught Maggie's attention just as she began to grease the hot skillet with suet. Quickly she opened the door, and Bowser shot past, nearly bowling her over. Gray Tabby, shadowlike, slipped past also. Tabby soon found his nest on some old rags in a wooden box behind the stove.

The kitchen was getting warm from the crackling alders, so Maggie left the back entry door open. The sun had begun to redden the sky above the tall firs and ragged pines across the lake, silhouetting the trees eerily against the horizon. Maggie's eyes caught a black, hulking mass moving among the water weeds and lily pads just down the lake, where Allagash Stream entered the forest. The shape left the lake now and in the twilight seemed to drift across the pucker-brush next to the water. Soon it blended into the forest and was gone.

Was it a moose? Maggie had seen one once next to Moosehead Lake, outside the village of Laketon. Since she and Grandpa were beginning that very morning a two-day trip up Allagash Stream to visit logging camps, she'd ask him to stop long enough to help her look for moose tracks. But what if it was a bear? Maggie thought she'd best remind Grandpa to bring his gun.

She turned to the stove and finished greasing the old iron spider with the sizzling suet. Maggie stepped to the butcher block and lifted the meat cleaver from its hook with her right hand while her left hand reached for the smoked venison—but it was gone!

Maggie dropped to her knees and peered under the table where Bowser was merrily licking his chops. Maggie dove for his collar, but she only succeeded in striking her head on a dropleaf brace. The leaf of the table banged down across her shoulders, sending a cup, a plate, and silverware bouncing off her back. The china plate slivered into a million shards as the silver-ware scattered across the floor. Thankfully, Grandpa's prize mustache cup, made of heavy ironstone porcelain, was undamaged.

Bowser, poised at the door, was ready to dart through as Maggie finally managed to stand. She could see that it was no use to try to catch the rascal. "You dumb dog!" she screamed. On impulse, Maggie pitched the meat cleaver at his retreating hindquarters as, tail between his legs, a girl's best friend ran into the entryway. Bowser's "Yipe!" drowned the dull thud of the heavy steel cleaver, as the backside of the blade bounced off his rump and against the wall. He shot through the latched screen door, taking the wire mosquito netting with him into the yard.

The opposite door opened at that moment, and Grandpa stepped in carrying his lantern and a pail of fresh milk. He stared at the racing animal through the torn screen. "What in thunder got into your dog, Maggie?" Grandpa exclaimed, astonished.

"Bowser just ate our breakfast," Maggie stated indignantly, yet sheepishly, restraining her fury. "I . . . I guess he's wrecked the screen door, and I suppose it's my fault."

"Pup's got to eat," Grandpa chuckled. "Now you won't have to hook him any fish before we leave him with Jake. Jake'll catch him a fish or two for his supper this afternoon," he added philosophically.

"We . . . we're not taking Bowser on the trip?"

"Can't take an untrained young dog into the deep woods. If he got on the trail of a rabbit, we'd waste half a day gettin' him back. An' besides, some o' them loggin' teamsters would plug him with a rifle 'fore you could holler stop if he spooked their horses," he pointed out. "Now you just get another junk o' deer meat an' chop it up. I see your spider's hot."

Maggie brought up another piece of smoked venison with the dumbwaiter while Grandpa poured the milk into jars and sent it down to the cellar on the same shelf. Maggie chopped the deer meat on the butcher block while Grandpa ladled hot water from the reservoir into an enameled basin between the kitchen's two windows. He lathered up with a brush in a heavy mug and began to shave with his straight razor, carefully trimming around his mustache.

Maggie found that the kettle of potatoes she'd left to cook slowly over the dying fire the night before were now boiled soft, their skins split for easy peeling. So, as the meat sizzled in the pan, she sliced half a dozen small ones and tossed the slices in with the venison for hash. Hot tea for Grandpa and cold milk for Maggie completed their breakfast.

The meal done, Grandpa took down his Bible to silently read a chapter. Maggie, however, hurried upstairs to dress and roll up a blanket for the trip north on the Allagash River.

Chapter 3

Jake Beavertail

———————

Old Jacques "Jake" Beavertail was sitting cross-legged in a chair opposite Grandpa's rocker when Maggie returned to the kitchen with her bedroll. Beside him, to her surprise, crouched Bowser, his nose on Jake's knee, as the old trapper scratched the hound's ears. On the floor lay Jake's wicker willow backpack containing his few belongings.

Maggie watched this wizened, bearded, French-speaking man, who was part Abenaki. Jake, in fact, was more French than Indian, but since he had chosen the life of a trapper and woodsman, he appeared to be as much an Indian as the red men who roamed the forest before white folks came from Europe. This morning Jake wore moosehide moccasins, leather breeches, and a deerskin shirt laced in front with rawhide. The only sign of civilization about him was his felt hat, tossed carelessly on his pack. And the hat bore the ornaments of his wild life—gray eagle, red turkey, and blue heron feathers were pushed jauntily into the band.

But if Jake were an Indian in appearance, in actions he was a French gentleman. Maggie recalled how, when they had first met a week earlier, he'd doffed his broad-brimmed felt hat, sweeping his feathers in the dust as he had bowed. *"Bonjour, mademoiselle,"* he had exclaimed in delight, as if greeting an old friend.

"How do you do, Mr. Beavertail," Maggie had politely replied. She had held back from offering her hand, though, for fear this friendly, yet foul-smelling fellow would kiss her fingers with his tobacco-stained lips.

Now, as she entered the kitchen, "Good morning, Mr. Beavertail," Maggie hesitantly greeted him, hoisting her bedroll onto the table.

"So *c'est la* city girl, *la* firetop," chuckled Jake. "It is Maggie, *non?*"

"Ye-yes, I mean *oui*," stammered Maggie. Not ordinarily at a loss for words, Maggie was embarrassed at his reference to her red hair. And she decidedly was not a city girl. Maggie had traveled to a city only once—to Augusta with Mother. But to old Jake, who'd seldom been out of the woods, Grandpa later explained, two or three houses made a "city," especially if there was a store, a church, a school, or a post office nearby.

But now Grandpa was gone, evidently up the front stairs to pack his own things for the trip, so Maggie found herself alone with this odd man. "Can . . . may I get you something for breakfast, Mr. Beavertail?" Maggie asked, more to fill the silence than to be polite.

"Jake, he eat at home. But to drink, *non?*"

Jake wanted a drink! And Grandpa had no liquor, not even beer or hard cider, Maggie recalled. Grandpa Fuller, in fact, would not permit alcoholic beverages in his house. And he tolerated tobacco only in those friends whose long-standing habit made it impossible for him to send them outdoors to smoke or chew.

So clearly, Grandpa had made a grave mistake inviting Jake to live alone in their house for two days while tending the horses. He'd be drunk when they returned, she was sure. "I can fix you a cup o' tea," she offered. Then Maggie remembered the can of coffee that Grandpa kept for special guests right behind the tea box on the pantry shelf. "Or perhaps you'd prefer coffee?"

Jake grinned broadly, and Maggie caught a glimpse of his nearly toothless mouth, his few remaining molars broken and black. Disgust and pity mingled within her at the sight.

"*Café, oui!*" Jake exclaimed. "*Café, s'il vous plaît!* Jake, he no get *café* except when he visit Bill Fuller. Only tea at home—only tea at the lumber camps."

"Coffee—*café* it is," Maggie chirped, regaining her composure, glad that Jake's thirst was for coffee after all. She hurried to ladle a measure of coffee into the blue agate coffeepot Grandpa kept on the shelf behind the stove. She added hot water from the teakettle, then set the pot on the stove, directly over the firebox. She quickly shook the ashes out of the grate with the stove poker and added two more sticks of alder wood to make the pot boil sooner, though the kitchen was already too hot.

From the cupboard Maggie fished out a heavy ironstone mug like Grandpa's, only without a mustache lip. The coffee was now hot, so Maggie poured a cup and passed it to Jake.

Jake blew and puffed on the steaming, scalding, wonderful-smelling beverage, and Maggie could see that it was too hot to drink. "*Café*, she is *bien*, but *café avec du lait*, she is better," Jake exclaimed.

Maggie was amused at the way Jake mingled French and English and accented the last syllable of his words. But what could he want?

"Jake wants milk in his coffee," quietly explained Grandpa, who had entered the kitchen while Maggie was pouring the coffee. "There's nearly a pint of *lait* left from breakfast on the sideboard next to the dumbwaiter. Give it all to Jake. He doesn't get much milk back in the woods. Last time he tried t' milk a cow moose in calf, she kicked him clear over t' Mt. Katahdin," Grandpa said, winking at Jake.

"*Merci beaucoup*," murmured Jake as Maggie passed him the milk. He sipped for a moment, patting Bowser all the while. "This dog, he was as scared as a treed coon when Jake find him," he said at last. Jake fingered a flap of torn skin on Bowser's tender rump, and the hound quivered in pain, whimpering. "Something hit him big, big hard," he remarked with a tone of empathy that made Maggie shrink in shame for having lost her temper with the meat cleaver.

❧ ❧ ❧

"Jake's a very fine man, especially considering that he's had a lonely and hard life," Grandpa explained later as he and Maggie paddled across the early morning lake's mirrored surface toward the north branch of Allagash Stream.

"I can't help feeling sorry for him," mused Maggie. "He seems so poor—and so old. He must be, why, nearly ninety," she said, recalling the thin, gray-haired man with the tanned and wrinkled leathery skin they'd left petting Bowser moments earlier.

"And how old do you think I am?" archly inquired Grandpa with a laugh.

"You were—let's see—seventy-two your last birthday."

"Jake is not yet fifty-three," Grandpa answered, amused. "He's skinny and wrinkled, but I've kept my bones well-padded with potatoes and pork, beans and steak. I guess if I lived on dandelion greens, fiddleheads, and boiled coon I'd be skinny, too."

"I'll say," agreed Maggie. "But Grandpa, then Jake's almost young enough to be your son!"

"Let's not get personal," retorted Grandpa with an edge of irritation. Ready as he was to accept Jake as a hunting and fishing companion, he was not ready to receive him as family. "Say, look at that!" Grandpa suddenly changed the subject as he pointed with his paddle to a brown pile on the sand, just where the stream joined the lake. "Bear droppings, fresh this morning! Big one, too, I'd say." He pointed further off, to claw marks in a clay embankment, climbing toward the roots of a great old gnarled hemlock that leaned over the water.

"Grandpa, I saw it! I saw the bear!"

"Gorry!" exclaimed Grandpa. He dropped his paddle at his feet and grabbed his rifle, pulling its hammer back with a sharp click as he swung the muzzle toward a nearby thicket of small balsam firs. "Where? Where is the bear, Maggie? And keep the canoe steady!"

"Oh, I don't mean now," Maggie exclaimed. "That was just before sunrise when I went out to fasten the screen door. I did mean to tell you then, except for the trouble with Bowser. Then Jake came in, and I was fixin' him coffee and he was scolding me for hurtin' Bowser. I just forgot."

Grandpa uncocked his gun, laid it down, and resumed paddling.

Maggie's shoulders ached and her arms felt like lead after what seemed ages of dip-and-push, dip-and-push, dip-and-push with her paddle. Though hers was of light cedar, and the soft deerskin carefully wrapped on its handle gave the paddle a comfortable grip, it had grown heavy as the hours dragged by. Although Grandpa, arthritic in the hips and knees, could walk but a mile or two without stopping to rub himself with horse liniment, he seemed to know no limits with his arms and shoulders. He had peeled off his wool shirt, and his red wool undershirt was moist with sweat. Yet he seemed to feel no strain, as with his much larger paddle he kept their canoe swift and straight on its course mile after mile against the stiff current.

Finally, Grandpa let his paddle rest across the canoe and pulled out his silver pocket watch. "Nearly ten o'clock, an' we've been paddlin' since seven," he announced. "Let's take a break."

"I was beginning to wonder," Maggie answered, "if you ever rested."

"Let's aim for that sandbar." Grandpa pointed toward a strip of yellow sand stretching from a gravelly shore at the stream's next bend. He put his paddle back in the water, and granddaughter and grandfather paddled furiously to reach the place of promised rest.

Maggie hopped nimbly from the front of the canoe as soon as it hit the sand. Grandpa Fuller, however, remained seated, instructing her on her next move. "Haul the canoe up a ways," he said. "With me in back, it'll come pretty easy."

Maggie pulled, and as soon as the canoe was on the bar, with only one end still in the stream, she watched in disbelief as her grandfather, so powerful in paddling, struggled like an invalid to get himself out of the canoe. First he placed his paddle across the canoe for support. Then, hitching sideways crablike, he struggled with strong arms to drag his hips and legs, one at a time, across the gunnel and onto the sandbar. Then he stood, wincing in pain, as his legs, which for three hours had been cramped and folded in the narrow canoe, straightened.

"Grandpa, are you all right?" Maggie said at last.

"Fine, fine. It's just that my rheumatiz' won't let me skip like a young-un anymore. Now let's take ten minutes." He stretched out full length on his back on the sand, pulled his straw hat across his eyes, and at once began to snore.

After their short rest, they pushed off once more. "We'll quit for dinner at noon," Grandpa explained. "That should get us t' Cook Camp by four or so, so's I can check out the condition of their horses as they bring 'em in from the woods. Could be they'll need to bring a few down the loggin' trail to The Elms an' swap with a couple I've got in the barn that's ready to go back to work. They'll have supper ready by six o'clock, sharp—it'll be standard woods fare, baked beans an' fried pork, with all the cornbread an' molasses you can eat!"

"I can taste it already. What did we bring for dinner?"

"Some o' that boiled deer meat I had in the pantry an' some boiled potatoes from off the back of the stove, left from breakfast."

Grandpa's meals are certainly more fattening than Jake Beavertail's, Maggie thought. But after venison and potatoes for two weeks, she'd be happy to try Jake's boiled coon and dandelion greens. "What do the logging camps serve for breakfast?" she asked.

"Flapjacks with maple syrup an' butter—all you can eat!" Grandpa seemed hungry for a change, too.

"Why can't I make us some flapjacks for breakfast when we get back?" Maggie wanted to know. "We've got plenty of flour."

"Sure you can. I'm not fond of deer meat all the time, myself. Just thought it'd be easy for you not to have to figure out recipes. I know your Grandma had a cookbook somewhere."

"Grandpa, for shame! I've been cooking for years. I thought you knew that . . . Grandpa!" Maggie caught her breath and said no more. Among the expanse of water, lily pads, and swale grass filling a cove nearly hidden by overhanging spruces and cedars stood a bull moose feasting on grass and lily shoots.

"Easy does it," Grandpa exclaimed in a hoarse whisper. He paddled backwards and ground the canoe to a halt against the clay bank opposite the opening of the cove.

The moose raised its head, its huge, flat-bladed antlers draped with dripping green water vines and flapping lily pads. The great beast, up to his belly in water, shook his mighty head to free himself from the vines. He stared through huge brown eyes at the intruders, then, unhurried and confident of his superior strength, the animal ambled slowly toward the forest.

Maggie was surprised by the length of the moose's legs as the beast emerged from the water. Though its body was the size of a riding horse, its legs seemed much longer. And since its hind legs were jointed backwards like a cow's, it walked like a huge toy animal, as if its joints were tied loosely together by string.

"Lotta steaks in that critter," Grandpa remarked as soon as they were underway again. "If we'd 'a' been on our way home, I'd 'a' shot him, and we'd have enough meat for months, and for Jacques Beavertail, too."

"Grandpa, you wouldn't!" Maggie was shocked.

"How do you suppose I got the deer meat you've been eatin'?" he asked in a matter-of-fact monotone.

Maggie did not answer. *Beans and fried pork are going to taste real good for supper,* she decided right then.

Chapter 4

The Allagash

As Maggie and Grandpa pushed north along Allagash Stream she seldom saw hardwood trees. The elms, oaks, maples, and birches that grew along the fencerows of The Elms and lined the streets of Laketon were almost entirely absent. Here, deep in the woods, the forest was nearly all evergreen. Spruce and hemlock overhung the stream. Here and there a majestic white pine, a remnant of the forest growing when the Pilgrims landed, waved majestically above the firs. Clumps of khaki-green cedars crowded the gullies and gorges that led away from Allagash Stream.

"Grandpa," Maggie inquired, "why do we see so many hardwood trees around villages and farms but so few in the forest?"

"Where villages and farms stand today, not just in Maine but in all of New England, pine forest once stood. Then, only a few hardwood trees were found here and there," he explained.

"But what happened to the pines?" Maggie asked.

"The pines were cut for lumber and ships' masts, though in the early days many trees were simply burned to get them out of the way. Hardwoods will spring up much quicker in the open fields and along fences than evergreens. But here in the deep woods, where the land was not clear cut, spruce, hemlock, and fir—all evergreens—have largely replaced the white pine. But if the forest is left undisturbed, pine will dominate after a century or so," said Grandpa.

Maggie noticed, too, that where the stream's bottom was sandy the water flowed clear and clean beneath them, not murky like the lake's water. It was so crystal clear that she could see the details of the patterns on the speckled trout swimming near the bottom, though several feet beneath them.

And from time to time, Maggie noticed, Grandpa would dip his blue agate drinking cup in the stream, drinking deeply to quench his thirst or splashing his nearly bald head with the water to cool off. "Mother told me never to drink from streams or brooks, no matter how clean they seem," Maggie remarked after Grandpa had done this several times. "She said I could catch typhoid fever and die."

"That's true, of course, unless you are upstream from all human settlements, since humans carry human diseases. I wouldn't even drink from Allagash Lake, since our house and barn both pollute it."

"But the lumber camps? You said some of them have over a hundred men living there."

"There aren't any lumber camps on this stream," Grandpa explained. "Chemquasabamticook Camp, where we're headin', is on the watershed that drains north, into the Piscataquis River and on into the St. John, then on east, then finally south into the Bay of Fundy, hundreds of miles from here in Canada. But Allagash Stream runs south, into our lake—and there are no people living above us."

"But how could our stream run south and Chemquas . . .—whatever—run north?"

"Simple. We've got t' portage over a ridge to the next stream this afternoon. That ridge is the north watershed, an' it drains into Chemquasabamticook Stream and Lake," Grandpa chuckled. "Allagash Stream takes the drainage from the south side of that same ridge."

"I thought you said this morning that we are going to Cook's Camp?" Maggie was puzzled.

"Cook Camp," Grandpa corrected. "That's short for Chemquasabamticook—that's an Abenaki Indian name."

"Oh!" Maggie expressed relief at this enlightenment. Grandpa's talk had made it sound like they would try to visit *two* lumber camps that very afternoon.

The portage took Maggie and Grandpa along a trail leading over a rocky ledge with low-growing ground hemlocks. Though earlier in the day Maggie had removed her shoes and socks to cool off, she stopped at once by the first clump of these low-growing prickly shrubs. "Let me get my shoes on, Grandpa. My shins'll be raw before we get ten feet if I don't get protection."

"Then you wouldn't wonder why their leaves are called needles," Grandpa chuckled. "I guess I can feel sorry for women-folk like you who wear dresses in the woods. When I was a kid I went barefoot in knee pants, an' I got more scratches than the hound who tackled the porcupine. But your high-top shoes ought to do the trick." He rested on a boulder while Maggie laced her high shoes.

Maggie led the way along the trail over the ridge, tugging on the canoe as Grandpa pushed from behind, sliding it where the ground was smooth and grassy, carrying it where it was rocky. They entered a thicket of poplars near the bottom of the ridge. In a huge anthill, a pair of partridges dusting themselves flew into the trees with a wild fluttering that nearly caused Maggie to drop her burden. "There goes some tasty game. An' my hands are full and I can't raise my gun," remarked Grandpa, as the fat birds disappeared among the trees. "But they'll eat buds in these poplars all fall and get fatter still. Maybe I'll come back in October and pick off a dozen with my double-barrel."

"Grandpa, do you really think all animals are for shootin'?" protested Maggie.

Grandpa was silent for a moment. Then he answered deliberately and carefully, "God gave us animals to eat, if we don't abuse the privilege. I know that some folks think that humans and animals are all one and that it's wrong to take animal life, especially if it's wild. But frankly, I can see no difference between killing a chicken and eating it and killing a partridge, if it's done with restraint. And I do enjoy eating wild game. Don't you?"

"Yes," admitted Maggie.

Aware that he had made his point, Grandpa wisely dropped the subject.

Beyond the poplar thicket the terrain abruptly flattened out, and the earth became soggy and boggy beneath their feet. The path now led through alders, which did not tower high above them like the poplars but reached just over their heads, the branches interwoven in a tangled mass that made a green canopy with a patch of blue here and there. Because the path was now overgrown with swale grass and hard to follow, Grandpa took the lead, and soon they were at the edge of the murky, boggy stream that would lead them into Lake Chemquasabamticook.

Maggie spied Cook Camp as soon as their canoe rounded the last clump of alders and slid out into the lake. Though it was nearly an hour's paddling away, far down the lake, she could see a tall plume of steam and smoke that rose from one building, larger than the rest, on a low hill above the camp. "That's the pumphouse and laundry," said Grandpa. "They've got a boiler, a steam pump, an' a reg'lar Chinese steam laundry in there to wash the men's clothes an' beddin'. Company's brought a Chinaman all the way from Boston to run it, too. This place is a reg'lar city. Y' see that long, low buildin' next t' the laundry? That's the dinin' hall, where we'll eat our supper with the men."

As they drew nearer, Maggie could see that though a few of the smaller buildings were log cabins, most were rough board structures covered with black tarred paper, which was held in place by slabs sawn off the sides of logs, the bark still on.

"That's why they call these loggin' camps slab cities," Grandpa remarked.

"But I'd think the roofs would leak," Maggie protested.

"They do, after a couple o' winters," Grandpa admitted. "But then, two, three years they move the entire camp. What they can haul off, they skid on an iced road with horses in the winter. The bunkhouses an' the large buildings they just leave t' rot into the ground. So you can see they can't build 'em very fancy. Costs too much."

A huge pile of logs, Maggie noticed, stood under a bluff, next to the lake. As she watched, a steady line of men, leading teams of heavy-hooved workhorses, drew logs from the woods, one or two at a time with each team. They unhitched their logs at a ramp leading to the pile then, riding standing up on the heavy sled used to hold the front end of the log out of the dirt, the men drove their teams to the paddocks. There the horses drank from a trough while being unharnessed. Meanwhile, sweating men with stout-handled peaveys equipped with steel cant hooks rolled the logs over the ramp to drop on the pile below.

"They just bring out a log or two when they come in from the woods for the night," Grandpa explained. "They spend all day twitchin' logs from the brush with their horses, an' they put 'em in small piles, where after the snow falls this winter they can load them onto pungs and haul them on ice-covered roads to the lake. In the spring when the ice thaws on the lake, the river drivers will move the logs down the stream to the sawmill on a railroad siding."

Maggie and Grandpa ate that evening at the head table with the woods' boss, a tall, muscular, handsome man with black hair. Maggie would not have been surprised to learn that he was Paul Bunyan himself; he even wore wide, red suspenders, Maggie noticed. He spoke English fluently, with only a slight tendency to heavily accent his final syllables, giving a musical French flavor to his speech.

The food was better than Maggie had imagined— her choice of three kinds of baked beans: yellow-eye, Jacob's cattle, or kidney beans; pork, cut thick and fried tender (not the leathery loin chops that Mama sometimes cooked in Laketon when she cooked only for Maggie and herself); corn bread, sweet molasses (Mama always bought strong blackstrap molasses, since it was cheaper), tea, and milk.

Though these men were rough and boisterous before entering the dining hall, as they sat on long, backless benches in their denim summer pants and plaid shirts of red or green, sleeves rolled to expose long red or gray union suits, they seldom spoke, except to ask for food. Here and there Maggie's *Anglais* ears caught a polite *s'il vous plaît* or *merci* as the platters of pork and earthenware pots of beans made their rounds.

Seated on a low stool at the end of this long hall, a white-haired old gentleman in a knitted, tasseled wool cap bent over an accordion, smoking a long clay pipe as he played, his tassel swinging in rhythm with his pumping and pulling. His melodies were sad, slow, melancholy yet certainly soothing, Maggie thought, to the nerves of men who had faced danger from falling trees or who had teamed sweaty horses all day long. The music relaxed her, also, for her excitement at the many new sights and sounds at the lumber camp had made it difficult for her to eat, and she had been sure she would not be able to sleep.

Though Maggie did not recognize the tunes, she imagined that the old musician wept at his sad strains as he played, though she could not be certain in the dim, sputtering light of the hanging kerosene lamps. She guessed that the words of the songs that seemed to so move the old musician were melodies of old Quebec or even of faraway France, as the scenes of his youth, the hardships of his lonely life in the woods, or perhaps memories of a dead wife or a lost child came back to the musician's mind.

"Who . . . who is that sad old accordion player, Grandpa?" Maggie whispered in awe when there was a lull in his conversation with the woods' boss.

"That's Gerard Bouchard. He's the cook's father, and he stays with her. He was a logger until he got too old to do heavy work," Grandpa answered quietly. "Now he does odd jobs and furnishes entertainment in return for a small pension and his room and board. He's all alone except for his daughter.

"There are many sad stories among the men who work in these loggin' camps," Grandpa softly added. "You'll learn a few of them by the time you've been in the woods a while."

Chapter 5

Marie

_____

Early on the morning of Maggie's second day in the woods she and Grandpa had flapjacks and maple syrup with the men in the dining hall. After breakfast, Maggie watched in surprise as Grandpa helped one of the loggers load their canoe aboard a heavy, high-wheeled, horse-drawn wagon. "Toss in your gear an' hop aboard," Grandpa called, as she stood there, puzzled.

Though the wagon was nearly full of axes, chains, leather harnesses, barrels of water, and bags of oats for the horses, with the canoe turned upside-down on top of it all, Maggie found a niche for her bedroll and climbed onto a bag of oats and sat down. "Gee-hup!" cried the driver, and the horses were off at a trot for the woods.

"This here's the supply wagon," Grandpa shouted above the rattle of wheels and the creaking of the harness from his perch on the seat beside the driver. "It will take us to the head of Thoroughfare Brook, since the loggers are working there today. From there it's downstream all the way to Eagle Lake, so we'll make good time. We'll visit Eagle Lake Camp this afternoon and spend the night there."

"Where are we going tomorrow?" Maggie wanted to know.

"Home! Eagle Lake Camp is south of here, down the lake and only a few miles east of Allagash Lake. Tomorrow morning we'll have 'bout an hour's portage 'cross the neck from Eagle to Chamberlain Lake, then about two hours paddlin' up Allagash Stream from Chamberlain to our lake, I figure. An' if we're lucky, we can catch a ride on North Woods' tugboat, which takes only an hour, so we won't have to paddle. I'm sure you remember Chamberlain Lake—we came that way when I brought you up from Laketon."

"So what are you doin' at Eagle Lake Camp?"

Grandpa grinned merrily. "Same thing's at Cook Camp. But there's some folks there I think you'll want to meet. We'll get there in good time for you t' visit before supper."

❦ ❦ ❦

"I didn't realize Eagle Lake Camp was so near our home at The Elms," Maggie said hours later, as she and Grandpa pointed their canoe toward the beach of Eagle Lake, just under the hill from the lumber camp, which looked to Maggie much like Cook Camp. As the canoe ground to a halt on the gravelly beach, Maggie spied a bare-legged, black-eyed girl eyeing them intently from the boulder which served as a stepping-stone up the embankment to the camp on high ground.

"Your face, it look like a toad that got too much sun."

Maggie stared in horror and pity at the imp who'd just uttered the insult. She was a skinny girl, taller than Maggie, but about her age. She slid off the boulder where she had been perched watching with interest as Maggie and Grandpa Fuller beached their canoe at Eagle Lake Camp. Maggie took in this scrawny, saucy kid with a swift glance as the girl approached. She wore too-small boy's corduroy knickers, tied at the waist with a rawhide thong. Her too-large feet were bare, and by her broken nails and tanned legs she had obviously worn neither shoes nor stockings since early spring. The rest of her clothing consisted only of a sleeveless, tattered loose buckskin shirt.

The girl's hair, black and straight, was waist length, and its only ornament was a bunch of soft bluebird feathers, which, tied with thread, held two thin braids pulled back from the sides to fall down in back. *Cute*, thought Maggie, for the moment forgetting the insult. *If she could dress as well as she fixes her hair, she would certainly improve her looks.*

"So you're *Grand-père* Fuller's red-haired brat grandkid. I've heard about you from the men on the tugboat. They say that when they stop at the horse farm for drinking water, you run off an' hide. Too good for us Frenchies, are you?"

What the girl said was partly true, and that caused Maggie's anger to rise as her freckles grew redder still. One day when two men came ashore from the tugboat, Maggie had simply decided that she preferred her privacy to the company of rough men who swore and spat tobacco juice. So she had slipped through the back kitchen door and had gone to her room where she listened through her floor register as the men talked with Grandpa. But one of them had no doubt seen the flash of her fire-red hair as she disappeared into the back hall, and this had evidently given the man something to make jokes about when he had returned to Eagle Lake Camp.

"An' you're wearin' shoes, like a city girl," the bold stranger continued. "'Round here only the men wear shoes, 'cause they have to work. *Les femmes et les filles* go barefoot. And such a pretty dress—expensive, *non*?" The strange girl brushed her fingers over Maggie's sleeve.

"It's only cheap calico," defended Maggie.

"I'll bet you've got a gingham one at The Elms—a silk one, too, no doubt. But they'd be too good to wear to a lumber camp, *non*? An' you're wearin' lacy bloomers under that fancy dress, like *les femmes en* Quebec, ain'tcha?" the girl accused.

"I'm wearing—" Maggie stopped, remembering that nice girls don't tell strangers what they have on under their dresses. She eyed the oddly dressed girl for a moment. "I'm wearing knickers, like you," she finally blurted out. "Who'd wear bloomers on a canoe trip?"

"Maggie, this is Marie LaRochelle. And Marie, this is my granddaughter, Maggie," interrupted Grandpa, who all the while had been watching Maggie's rude welcome to Eagle Lake Camp with concerned amusement.

"How do you do," Maggie said with a politeness she had learned from Mother in Laketon. To tell the truth, Maggie's greeting sounded every bit as stiff and stuck-up as Marie expected of an *Anglaise* girl like Maggie. And Maggie was at once sorry, for, despite Marie's insults, she was beginning to find her interesting.

"Hi," responded Marie. "Meet Gilbert." With that she flipped open a fold in the hem of her leather top, revealing a huge, warty toad, which she tossed, squirming and kicking, at Maggie.

Maggie didn't flinch. Instead she caught the flopping, cold-skinned amphibian, though it felt horrid in her hands. "Gilbert, I'll bet Marie loves you like I love Bowser," she said, petting the ugly creature with pretended affection.

"Toad'll pee on your fingers an' you'll catch his warts, which is 'most 's bad 's havin' freckles," squealed Marie in delight.

"In that case, you can have him back." Maggie flung the toad.

"I don't want no stupid toad, anyway," Marie snapped, catching him then gently setting him down. "C'mon, I'll show you where you're sleepin' tonight," she added with an abrupt change of demeanor. Before Maggie could pick up her bedroll by its leather strap, Marie had grabbed it. "I'll carry it. You're the guest," she said curtly, tossing it onto her shoulder and striding off toward a small, low building near the camp's dining hall.

Maggie looked at Grandpa for advice. "Better go with her," he said. "Marie's the cook's daughter. I'm sure you're expected to share her room tonight."

Just outside the dining hall two loggers were perched on stools made of upturned logs. They were carefully filing the teeth of their crosscut saws as Maggie and Marie approached.

"*Sacrebleu!*" one exclaimed to the other. "Here is *la* half-breed squaw-*fille* Marie with that fire-top *Anglaise fille*—the one the tugboatmen were telling about, *non*? Did you ever see such a sight, *non*? The squaw-girl will be too fine to speak to us ordinary folks if she spends much time with the English girl," he said. The men continued to chuckle and exchange comments in French as the girls passed.

"Is everyone at Eagle Lake Camp that *polite*?" asked Maggie as soon as they were inside the cabin Marie shared with her mother.

"Never mind the men," replied Marie. "Besides my mother, you 'n' me's the only *filles* or *femmes* they have seen for months. And your hair *does* attract attention."

"I hate my hair! Why did I have to be born with red hair?" Maggie moaned.

"Actually, it's beautiful—deep red like that—you'd win beauty contests *en* Quebec. Mine's—well, rather ordinary."

"Your hair is beautiful, too. And I like the way you've fixed it with those feathers!"

"You like, eh? Maybe I can help you with yours, *non*?"

Maggie was suddenly aware that her shoulder-length hair, though naturally wavy, was a tangled mess from canoeing all day with Grandpa with no time to comb since early morning. "Do you have a brush?"

"Sure. Help yourself." Marie pointed to a hairbrush on a washstand beneath a hanging wall mirror. "Mother 'n' I share that one."

The brush, Maggie noticed as she picked it up, had more blonde hairs caught in it than black. "You said your mother uses this?" she asked hesitantly. Maggie certainly did not expect this dark-haired girl's mother to be blonde.

"My *maman's* blonde. Lots of French *femmes* are," Marie explained. "My *père* was half Abenaki. That makes me one-fourth Indian, but I guess I got all of Father's Indian blood—that's what my *maman* says."

"Is . . . is your *père*—your father—alive?"

"No. He died when I was four. I can barely remember him."

"You're lucky," answered Maggie.

"Meaning?" Marie's voice was tinged with anger.

"I . . . I mean you're lucky to have known your father. I never knew mine. He died before I was born," Maggie explained.

"Oh! I guess I should sympathize with you, oughtn't I? I'm so sorry. An' I didn't mean t' be mean when you and *Grand-père* Fuller landed in your canoe."

"Your *maman*—your mother—she hasn't remarried, has she?" asked Maggie as she worked out her snarls with the brush.

"No, she hasn't. She says one man in a lifetime is all she could take."

"My mother remarried. I have a stepbrother, and he's just my age. That's why I'm living with Grandpa. Mama's house wasn't big enough for both of us." It was now Maggie's turn to be upset.

"This house ain't very big—only one room, besides my sleeping loft," Marie ventured, pointing to a ladder leading to planks across the ceiling beams above. "It's a small loft, but if you think it's too crowded, I'll just sleep with *Maman*," she said, nodding toward the double bed that took up nearly a third of the cabin's main floor. "We eat in the kitchen in the other buildin', an' we take baths there, too, after hours. The camp laundry does our wash, which is lucky, 'cause *Maman's* so busy cooking for the crew that she couldn't find time to wash clothes."

Maggie and Marie soon found Marie's *maman*, Evangeline LaRochelle, preparing supper for a crew of more than two hundred hungry men in the camp kitchen in a wing of the dining hall. *Madame* LaRochelle was a small woman—a *petite femme*, is how Marie described her—who wore her blonde hair, which was waist length like her daughter's, in a long, single braid tied with a rawhide thong. When the girls spied her at work, *Madame* LaRochelle was standing on bare tiptoes on a stool, stirring a boiling copper kettle of soup, one of several huge kettles on a long stove, larger than any kitchen range Maggie had ever seen.

"*Maman*," cried Marie, "*mon amie*, she is Maggie!"

Madame LaRochelle turned around. "Maggie, I've heard about you. *Est-ce que vous êtes la petite-fille de Monsieur Guillaume* Fuller's, *non*?"

"*Excusez-moi, s'il vous plaît?*" Maggie answered, trying to make herself understood to this French Canadian woman. "What did you ask?"

"So you don't *parlez français*," *Madame* LaRochelle answered with a merry laugh. "But I speak English, so we can communicate, *non*? And William Fuller, he is your *grand-père, non*?"

"*Oui*—I mean, yes," Maggie answered quickly, taking in Marie's mother in a glance. *Madame* LaRochelle wore an ankle-length denim dress, hemmed with lace, and over this a white bibbed apron, which like her dress was trimmed in lace and heavily embroidered. Though spattered with soup, the apron was evidently a work of art. Her bare feet were dainty and small, quite unlike Marie's long ones, though they were calloused from long hours of work on the rough plank kitchen floor.

Evangeline LaRochelle's eyes were pale blue, exactly matching her denim dress. Her eyes struck Maggie at once. Evangeline was beautiful, the bloom of youth still on her rosy cheeks, but her eyes were sad, like the eyes of a caged animal of the forest which had lost its right to roam.

"Marie is showing me around Eagle Lake Camp," Maggie said, once she'd caught her breath from taking in the beauty of Marie's young mother. Maggie paused and sniffed.

"The soup, it is *bien*—good—no?" *Madame* LaRochelle inquired.

"The soup smells delicious. I can see you must be very busy."

"I like my work," said Evangeline. "Come back in about an hour, and you can taste it."

"If we come back in half an hour, can we help put the food on the tables, *Maman*?" Marie asked.

"*Oui*—yes. Does Maggie wish to help?"

"*Oui*, of course," Maggie chirped.

"And Marie, put a dress on," Evangeline sternly instructed. "In that outfit, you look like, how they say it *en anglais*—a ragamuffin. I keep telling you, knickers are for *les garçons*." She winked at Maggie, who grinned back. "Boys wear britches; girls wear dresses," she chuckled.

❦ ❦ ❦

"Maggie has invited me to spend a week with her at the horse farm," Marie remarked that evening as the girls sat in their nightgowns with their legs dangling over the edge of Marie's loft above her mother's bed.

Evangeline put down the book she was reading beneath a kerosene lamp, the only light in the cabin. She uncurled herself from the old chair and peered at the two pairs of eyes that twinkled, owl-like, from the shadows under the roof rafters. "What does *Grand-père* Fuller say to that?"

"He thinks it's a great idea," put in Maggie. "He says I've been a grouch lately, an' maybe I need someone my own age to play with."

"I can ride back to camp across Allagash Lake on the tugboat any day I choose," Marie added. "You can do without me for a few days, can'tcha, *Maman*?"

"I'm not sure what *Grand-père* Fuller will do with you two scamps," Evangeline fussed. "My *maman* used to say that one *fille* will do the work of half a *femme*, two *filles* will do the work of half a *fille*, and three *filles* are as helpful as no *fille* at all."

"We'll do the work of *two* girls," Marie and Maggie responded in unison.

"Like at supper tonight. Maggie's help was cleaning up Marie's messes," *Maman* LaRochelle teased. "Now I'm going to read another chapter, then I'm blowing out the lamp. You *filles* roll up in your blankets and go to sleep."

As Evangeline picked up her brown, leatherbound book again, Maggie thought she could see its title on the spine. Though she could read only a few words of French, it looked like a Bible.

Chapter 6

A Forest School

Reading *McGuffey's Eclectic Reader* and doing written exercises in *Harvey's Grammar* was not Maggie's idea of spending a sunny Monday morning in September at The Elms. But she had made a deal with Grandpa Fuller upon his decision to let Marie come home with them for a week. Since it was the first week in September, and school started in Laketon on the first Monday of the month, Maggie had promised to study at least two hours a day, even though she had a guest.

"I went to school in Quebec for a couple of years," Marie said wistfully, when Maggie had apologized for the fifth time, at least, about having to spend two hours in her books. "I can't read *anglais*—not very well, anyway—but I'm sure you can teach me. Then we'll have a *real* school, and you'll be the teacher."

"If you went to school in French," asked Maggie, puzzled, "how can I teach you in English?"

"*Maman* can read both French an' *anglais*. Sometimes she gets a copy of the newspaper to read when the camp boss is done with it. I can always figure out a few of the words in English, an' sometimes even make out a sentence," Marie said.

Maggie was not convinced. But she did have to work Marie into her school schedule somehow, for that week at least. And she was pleased with the idea of becoming a teacher. Grandma Fuller, Maggie had heard, had been a teacher in her own one-room country schoolhouse before her sixteenth birthday. At almost thirteen, Maggie couldn't see why she couldn't do the same.

"Tell y' what," Maggie suggested, "you read me a story from the reading book. I'll help with the words when you get stuck. That way we'll get our lessons together."

When Maggie had decided to live with Grandpa, and Mama had finally granted her permission, Mama had assembled a collection of schoolbooks in an old wooden soapbox. Some of these books had been in the Ridlon or Fuller families for generations. And since both Grandma Ridlon and Grandma Fuller had been schoolteachers for several years before they were married, Mama also found several teachers' editions of these textbooks in the attic with the other books.

Into the box went a complete set of *McGuffey's Eclectic Readers*, spelling book and all. When Maggie protested, "Mama, I've read the *Primer* and the first four *Readers*. All I'll need is the *Fifth* and *Sixth*," Mama was determined that she take them all, since the books were a set. "I want these books all kept together, so's they don't get lost," Mama firmly stated. She packed also *Harvey's Grammar and Composition*, both the elementary and secondary editions. "Since you're 'mos' ready for grammar school, which is almost high school, you'll likely be in the secondary book before the year's out," Mama explained. *Harper's Geography, Ray's Complete Arithmetic, Spencer's Penmanship*, and Morris and

Leigh's history of the United States, *The Great Republic*, completed the set.

Maggie had complete confidence in Grandpa Fuller as a tutor. He'd finished eight grades in school, in those days a complete education for a backwoods boy whose parents could not afford to send him to a boarding academy. But he'd taught himself geometry, trigonometry, and the basics of civil engineering. For much of his adult life, he had worked as a surveyor, the noble profession of George Washington before he became a soldier.

Grandpa's bookcase at The Elms contained the grandest library Maggie could imagine. Even the Laketon library's musty collection of novels and biographies failed to approach Grandpa's selection. Maggie counted more than two hundred books, and as evening by evening she read from these, she found them full of notes in Grandpa's own handwriting. Truly her grandfather was a learned man, Maggie concluded.

"Let's start with the *Third Reader*," Maggie suggested. She believed Marie would probably read only from the *First* or *Second Readers*, but that sounded babyish, and Maggie felt that she herself would be bored with the books for the younger children. "An' since it's such a nice day, let's study outdoors, down by the big rock." *Study*. That was a nice-sounding word. Maggie had wanted to say "read," but Grandpa said they were to be in school for at least two hours, so "study" sounded much more appropriate. Clutching the *Reader*, Marie scampered after Maggie toward the boulder by the lakeside.

"That's an Indian turnip—what you *Anglais* call a jack-in-the-pulpit, isn't it?" Marie said moments later, pointing to a single straight stem covered with red berries growing beside Maggie's big rock. "That's an *arisema triphyllum*. And see, it grows on the north side of the boulder!"

The Elms' house faced east, toward the lake, so Maggie knew that the left-hand side of the rock was north. "How did *you* know that?" Maggie asked in surprise. "And you called it a jack-in-the-pulpit?" Maggie added, puzzled. "It looks like a memory root plant to me."

"The *arisema triphyllum* always grows in the shade when it's found in the open, outside the woods," Marie responded confidently. "Too much sun will kill them, and the shade is on the north side of the rock, of course. The jack-in-the-pulpit is a forest plant. It's also called an Indian turnip, 'cause the Abenaki like to boil the roots and eat them. Its blossom, which comes out in April, is the jack-in-the-pulpit, which you'll see next spring."

"But what is the French name you called it?" Maggie insisted.

"Not French. Latin. *Maman* likes to study flowers, birds, animals—everything that lives. Whenever she can get a book on wildlife she studies it and teaches me their scientific names. But why do you call it a memory root?"

"Because it's *hot*!" Maggie exclaimed. "If you taste it once, you'll remember it! No wonder Indians don't wear many clothes if they eat that stuff."

"I'm an Indian," Marie answered hotly. "I've eaten them, an' they're not hot!"

"I'm sorry." Maggie tried hard to keep from laughing. "Really I am." Maggie knew she *was* sorry she had hurt Marie. She had shared Marie's silent anger when the woodcutters had teased her and called her a squaw-girl. But Marie's sudden switch from being a French girl to calling herself an Indian—after spouting strange Latin words—had taken Maggie by surprise.

"So you think that's funny! You *Anglais* are all the same—you look down on us Abenaki. If that's the way you feel about it, I'm jumpin' aboard the tug next time it comes down the lake for a load o' logs." Marie was so angry now that she was almost in tears.

"That's certainly not true! Grandpa's very best friend, Jake Beavertail, is Abenaki, an' he visits with us often," Maggie protested.

The girls' discussion had grown loud. Grandpa, who had been on the verandah whittling a new axe handle from a piece of white ash, silently shuffled up on his slow, arthritic legs. "You girls are both right, but you are both wrong to be angry," he said, trying to help them find a point of agreement.

Marie glared at Mr. Fuller, but she was willing to listen respectfully to what Maggie's *grand-père* had to say. Maggie, for her part, watched Marie in concern and worry, yet she was relieved to have someone else to take the heat.

"The jack-in-the-pulpit is an Indian turnip," Grandpa mildly remarked.

"See! Told ya," Marie fairly screamed.

Grandpa held up his hand for silence. "Maggie is also right—that plant's root will make yer mouth smart somethin' wicked if y' eat it without *cookin'* it first. Even though I'd be unhappy to pull up a jack-in-the-pulpit just t' prove a point, if you girls wish to quarrel, I shall do just that." He stepped toward the plant with his whittling knife.

"Grandpa, no! Please don't," Maggie cried. "Please don't dig it up."

Grandpa turned and smiled wryly at Marie. "Do *you* want to taste it?"

"No, not really. It's just that since I've never eaten a raw one, I figured they'd taste all right, like cooked ones."

"When I was a boy," said Grandpa, "I learned about Indian turnips the way a lot o' kids used t' learn such things—by experience. We had a neighbor who boiled and ate 'em. So I bit right into a raw one, and it set my mouth on fire. My tongue smarted for two days, seemed like!"

"But have you ever eaten them cooked?" Marie insisted.

"Oh, yes. Many times. Sometimes in the spring Jake Beavertail will show up at my kitchen door with his knapsack full o' Indian turnips and fiddlehead greens. I enjoy eatin' both with him, of course. But when I tell Jake that there's comin' a time when the jack-in-the-pulpit will no longer be plentiful, he just says if it was left t' the Abenakis, there'd always be plenty t' eat in the woods."

"That's true," Marie brightened.

"But I heard you call it an *arisena triphyllum*, by its Latin name. I've never heard that before. But y' see, even an old codger like me can still learn. Now you girls dig into your books," he chuckled, as he walked back to his whittling on the verandah.

Marie passed over several stories in the *Third Reader* that were illustrated by steel engravings of little girls in frilly dresses and boys in what seemed to her silly, citified clothes. After flipping over a few pages she found a picture of five, furry, flat-tailed creatures on a log, surrounded by willow and swamp trees with cat-tails growing out of the water around them. *"Les castors*—how you say in *anglais*? Beavers, no?" she chuckled.

Marie followed Maggie's instructions perfectly as she read, making corrections and rereading each sentence until she could say them without faltering, and Maggie successfully helped Marie read such long words as *curious, frequently,* and *constructed.*

Marie next found a story entitled, "The Young Teacher," about a boy whose father was teaching him to read and write. The boy, whose name was Charles, was using his playtime to teach another boy, the son of a poor fisherman, to read. The fisherman and his wife could not read, and they were too poor to afford to send their son to school, for in those days there were few free schools.

"That's like you 'n' me," Marie exclaimed, "'cept I have been t' school an' my *maman* can read. 'Course a real school'd be more fun, but I'm having fun right now."

"Wait'll we get to arithmetic," warned Maggie. "That's no fun. 'Course Grandpa's good at math, so I expect he can help us if we get stuck."

"I'm good at arithmetic, too," Marie assured her. "Arithmetic's the same in *anglais* as it is in French, ain't it?"

"I'm not sure," Maggie answered hesitantly. "But if it's different, Grandpa can figure it out. Have you had enough school for this morning? We can work on arithmetic this afternoon."

"*Oui*—yes," answered Marie. "But shall we walk along the lake, *non*?"

"Sure," said Maggie. She placed the reading book on the boulder, then carefully weighted it with a stone to keep the breeze from flipping its pages. Maggie whistled for Bowser, who had been scratching first one long ear then the other as he watched Grandpa at his whittling. "Marie and I want to walk part way around the lake. We'll only be gone a couple of hours. May we, Grandpa?" Maggie called.

"What are the rules of the woods?"

"If we get lost, travel downhill until we come to water. Then we can follow the lakeshore back to The Elms," Maggie recited.

"And what about the dog?"

"If Bowser strikes off after a rabbit or a squirrel, I'm not to try to follow him. He'll come home by himself."

"You've got it," Grandpa answered. "Now be back in time to finish your lessons before supper, hear?"

"I hear."

"Actually there's another good rule, if you're lost in the deep woods and can't see the sun on a cloudy day," Marie said, as girls and dog struck out across a point that separated The Elms from a small woodland cove on the lake.

"What's that?" Though Maggie was supposed to be educating her newfound friend in books, Marie's knowledge of nature had already impressed her.

"Moss always grows on the north side of trees an' large rocks."

"So?" Maggie asked. "Oh!" she suddenly said before Marie could answer. "If you know which direction north is, you can always walk in a straight line in any direction an' eventually come to civilization. I've heard that people sometimes get lost and walk in the woods until they die, 'cause they travel in circles."

"That's right," agreed Marie. "Even in the Allagash wilderness, if you travel in a straight line, you'll come out somewhere, sooner or later. West will take you to Quebec. South comes out in populated areas of Central Maine."

"And north?"

"North would take you to the big river, the St. John, an' you could make a raft and float to Fort Kent."

"You know the woods pretty well, don't you?" Maggie asked. "I guess you're like Grandpa. He says he'd rather live in these woods than a city any day. But," she confided, "a bear came by here a few days ago, a big one, Grandpa thinks. Suppose we meet a bear?" Maggie shuddered at her own words.

"Bears don't hurt nobody." Marie sounded sure of herself.

"What about the skeleton of the man they found beside the skeleton of a bear in that old log cabin over toward Mt. Katahdin last spring?" Maggie said. "I read about that in the newspaper." She was trying to sound calm, but even retelling the story made her nervous.

"I heard about that," Marie answered thoughtfully.

"Maybe the story wasn't true," replied Maggie, remembering that Mama and Grandpa had both once said that news reporters sometimes stretch the truth to sell more newspapers. "Yellow journalism," Mama had called it. "You gotta have a membership in the 'Liars' Club' before they'll hire you t' write for a newspaper," Grandpa had said.

"It was true, all right," Marie admitted. "One of the men from Eagle Lake Camp saw the skeletons."

"Then bears *are* dangerous!"

"Maine bears are dangerous only if you get them cornered," Marie explained. "This fellow who was killed was a city fellow. He'd gone off fishing alone, and when he came back to his cabin he found the bear in his food supply. A smart woodsman would've opened a window an' merely hollered in at the bear. The bear'd have gone out the door, an' that'd been the end of it. But this guy, he blocks the door with his body, then shoots the cornered bear. What could he expect a wounded bear trying to escape t' do?"

Maggie shuddered at the thought.

"*Les canards*," Marie said quickly and quietly. "*Mallarts!*" She pointed through the pines to the cove, now just ahead across a gravelly beach. The far side of the inlet was swampy, and dozens of black and brown birds, some of them with blue-green heads, bobbed and darted on the water.

"Mallard ducks," Maggie agreed, "lots of 'em— must be a couple hundred, at least."

"Quack, wack, wack, quack! Wack-wack-wack," Marie called.

"Ow-o-o-o-o-o-o," answered Bowser, bounding up to the girls' heels.

Maggie quickly grabbed her hound's muzzle and held it shut while she shushed him. "Grandpa says you'd make a fine bird dog, but not if you scare them off," she whispered.

Marie quacked in near-perfect imitation of a duck's call as Maggie and Bowser hunkered on their haunches and watched. Several ducks turned and paddled toward the near side of the cove. The others soon followed, and very quickly the entire flock was near the beach, just under the tree-covered knoll where the girls were watching.

"Arf!" Maggie had relaxed her grip on Bowser only for an instant. With a roar of what seemed like a million wings the mallards were in the air. Maggie held her breath as the ducks, in flawless formation, wheeled and flapped off down the lake.

"*Anatidae!*" exclaimed Marie in delight.

Marie's fancy Latin scientific names for mallard ducks, which she had learned from her mother, did not impress Maggie at the moment. Instead she was amazed by the beauty of the birds and at the grace with which they glided off.

❧ ❧ ❧

"Grandpa," Maggie asked that evening during supper at The Elms, "how could those ducks all fly the same direction in an instant without colliding into each other?"

"Tell me, too, *Grand-père*," put in Marie. "*Maman* and I are studying wildlife. But there's so much her books don't seem to tell."

"A wise poet once wrote," Grandpa pointed out, "that 'He, who from zone to zone, / Guides through the boundless sky thy certain flight, / In the long way that I must trace alone, / Will lead my steps aright.'"

"That's beautiful," exclaimed Maggie.

"More than beautiful," insisted Grandpa. "It's also true."

"Well, of course I know it's true," Maggie said, surprised. To her a poem was something to feel, not to think about. "But what do you *mean*?"

"Every one o' those ducks is guided by what we humans choose t' call instinct. Whether in sudden flight, like today when Bowser roused them, or in their long migrations in the fall and the spring, they go exactly where they're supposed t' go, without ever colliding, unless interfered with by an intruder."

"Like a hunter with a shotgun," Maggie said thoughtfully.

"William Cullen Bryant wrote those lines o' poetry after watching a waterfowl—perhaps a mallard duck or a Canada goose—fly south for the winter. Bryant realized that the power which guides the bird is more than mere instinct—or even what some call Mother Nature. It is God Himself. And when God is in control of our lives, we humans are not constantly colliding with each other."

"Like this morning when Maggie and I 'collided' over a silly disagreement, *non*?" Marie put in, pleased that she had mastered a new English word—*collided*—while learning a new truth, as well. Marie was pleased, also, that *Grand-père's* knowledge of nature went far beyond merely learning scientific facts.

Maggie was silent and thoughtful. This half-wild, part-Indian daughter of a lumber camp cook, who said *oui* for yes and called ducks *canards*, seemed to be learning more from Grandpa than she. Maggie, in fact, wondered if just maybe Grandpa was beginning to like Marie a bit more than he did her.

Chapter 7

The Chopping Contest

The weeks at The Elms went by, and Marie came and went every couple of weeks for a day or two. Maggie was teaching her to read English—*anglais*, Marie still preferred to call it. Grandpa Fuller was teaching both girls arithmetic. With her *maman's* help at Eagle Lake Camp, Marie soon finished the *Third Reader* and was halfway through the *Fourth*. She would soon catch up with Maggie, who was in the *Fifth Reader*. Maggie feared she would catch up with her in math, as well.

"Thanksgiving is the week after next," Marie said one day late in September, when she had come to The Elms to study with Maggie.

Maggie was about to disagree. Thanksgiving was in November, she knew. But by now she had learned that to disagree with Marie could lead to angry arguments. So instead she asked mildly, "Why is it early this year?"

"Thanksgiving in Canada, it is not early. American Thanksgiving, is late, *non*?" Marie answered.

"Oh. Canadian Thanksgiving is in October?"

"*Oui!* On the second Monday. And American, it is in November."

Maggie congratulated herself that she had avoided a quarrel with Marie, yet she was peeved to discover that, once again, Marie knew more than she did. Maggie, in fact, knew little about Canada, though she'd been around Canadians all her life. But Marie knew a lot about America—she could name the states, all thirty-eight of them, and the nine territories as well. And she knew about Lincoln and Washington. Marie even knew that Civil War hero Ulysses S. Grant was president of the United States.

Maggie, for her part, could name only three Canadian provinces, and she had no idea who was the prime minister of Canada. "So what happens on Canadian Thanksgiving Day?" Maggie finally forced herself to ask.

"We eat turkey an' cranberries an' pumpkin pie. *Maman* an' her helpers bake pies for three days before Thanksgiving."

To Maggie, this sounded much like American Thanksgiving.

"An' the chopping contest. Eagle Lake Camp competes with Cook Camp an' the other camps. Then the men find out who's the fastest pine log chopper in the entire Allagash Wilderness," Marie said enthusiastically.

"When my Grandpa Fuller was a young man he was the fastest man with an axe in the upper Kennebec Valley," Maggie answered. She did not feel this to be bragging, for she believed it to be true. Mama had said so, and she'd once heard an old man boast that "Ol' Bill Fuller can beat any chopper with an axe in the State o' Maine."

But Maggie was surprised and a bit embarrassed when, two days after Marie went home, the logging company's tugboat anchored offshore and two men lowered a rowboat and came ashore. They brought a letter from Eagle Lake Camp's boss.

"What's the letter about?" Maggie inquired, after Grandpa had read it through twice, trying to figure out the misspelled English words with which the French camp boss had written his note.

"We're invited for their Thanksgiving celebration," Grandpa answered with concern. "And we can hardly refuse, though it's the first time I've been asked t' come in all the years I've lived at The Elms. Seems that somehow they got wind o' the fact that I once won a log-choppin' contest at the Foxcroft State Fair. I was called the fastest man with an axe on the upper Kennebec," he said with a wry smile. "But that was more'n thirty years ago."

"But what do they want you to do?" Maggie was beginning to worry.

"They're adding a new feature this year—an old-timer's contest," he said.

"You're an old-timer," Maggie said with a sigh of relief. "Sounds all right to me."

"Maggie, an old-timer in these woods is anyone past forty. Most woodchoppers wear out by the time they're thirty—forty at the latest. They leave the woods to marry and become farmers or mill hands. Those who do stay usually work for the logging crews as horse handlers, saw filers, or maintenance men. If they're still choppin' wood, they're usually very tough!"

"Oh."

"'Oh,' is right. So I'd be competing with men twenty or thirty years younger—many young enough to be my kids. Old-timers, indeed!"

"G-Grandpa," Maggie stammered, "I *did* tell Marie you'd once been a champion chopper."

"That's all right, Maggie." Grandpa put his arm across her shoulders. "I'll just sharpen up my old choppin' axe—practice a bit. We'll show them fellows this ol' geezer has some life left in 'im yet!"

🍎 🍎 🍎

Maggie was out of bed long before dawn on Canadian Thanksgiving Day. Marie, who had spent the two previous days with her learning math and English, had kept Maggie awake much of the night, kicking her ribs with bony heels, though the wide bed was big enough for both girls.

Now the girls were dressing, taking turns brushing their hair in front of the mirror above Maggie's bedside table. Marie was wearing a new gingham dress. On her feet, too, were new brown leather high-cut shoes, which laced nearly to her knees. Though the Maine woods had had only a light dusting of snow that fall, Marie had finally agreed to wear the shoes her *maman* had ordered along with the cloth from Quebec City.

"We've got a little scheduling problem, I'm afraid," Grandpa said as he set down his pail full of Molly's Jersey milk after returning from the barn before breakfast. Maggie was turning the hot pancakes in Grandma Fuller's old cast-iron spider as Marie set the table.

"What do you mean?" Maggie asked.

"The first run-off of the old-timer's chopping contest is at eleven o'clock, accordin' to a message the camp boss sent me late yesterday. That means I've got to leave immediately after breakfast if I'm to get there on time in my canoe."

"We'll be ready," chirped impetuous Marie.

"Grandpa, there's not going to be many dirty dishes. We can have everything spic an' span in twenty minutes," Maggie assured him.

"That's not the problem. I told Jake Beavertail last week to be here at nine, since I didn't expect to compete until early afternoon. And there's no way to reach Jake to tell him to come earlier, since it's 'mos' a two-hour walk to his cabin."

"But Jake knows what to do," Maggie protested.

"Unfortunately," Grandpa sighed, "we've got a young mare in foal in the barn. She's about to give birth, and she may have complications. So I've got to leave some written instructions."

"That should take care of it," Maggie agreed.

"Trouble is, Jake can't read. So you an' Marie'll need to stick around till he gets here and read my instructions to him, then walk the trail around the lake. You'll be there in plenty of time for the afternoon semifinals, if you hustle. And remember, dinner's served at six. I do expect t' make the semis," he added confidently.

Chapter 8

The Shortcut

Maggie and Marie hurried along the old Indian trail toward Eagle Lake Camp. "Too bad the tug's not running today. We'd 'a' been there by now," Maggie grumbled.

"You're the one who's always lookin' for new experiences. This is a new experience, *non*?" Marie joked.

"Have you been this way before?" asked Maggie.

"'Course not. I always go partway by canoe, partway by tugboat, an' portage between Chamberlain an' Eagle Lake. But if this trail goes east around the north side of Allagash Lake, like your *grand-père's* map shows, we'll come out by the tug landin' on Eagle Lake, right where I left my canoe the day 'fore yesterday."

"Well, let's check the map. We're at a fork in the trail." Maggie pointed to the path ahead, where a wellworn trail led uphill to the north. But the trail straight ahead became faint, though it led downhill and east, in the direction Marie said they should go.

"Silly. I've told you already if we just go east we'll get there okay. We can't miss a long *lac* like Eagle Lake."

71

"But Grandpa's map shows that we are to take the *left* fork at this point—that's north," insisted Maggie. "Then it shows us swingin' back east again after we get around a bog."

"Why do you s'pose there's a trail leadin' straight into the bog?" Marie persisted. "Some trails are part-year trails, an' this here's one o' those. Durin' the October drought it dries up, an' durin' winter the trail is frozen. *Grand-père* wanted us to choose the best route for ourselves, I'm sure." Marie started downhill, toward the bog.

"Marie!" Maggie was angry.

Marie paused and turned.

"Grandpa's map *distinctly* shows us goin' north here!"

Marie shrugged. "Suit yerself. But this's a shortcut that'll get us there at least an hour sooner. An' it's easier walkin'—why climb over all that brush on the high trail?"

"I . . . I don't know."

"S'pose *Grand-père* loses the first contest. You wouldn't get to see him compete at all."

Maggie was convinced at last. She *did* wish to watch Grandpa chop, even if he lost. Since he would no doubt be the oldest chopper in the contest, she could be proud of him for even trying. So she raced after Marie toward the swamp, Bowser bounding joyfully behind.

By the time the girls had reached the level ground of the boggy bottomland, the sky was overcast. "Think it's goin' t' rain?" Maggie worried.

"Naw. Cloud cover's not heavy enough. This'll cool things down for the choppin' contest, though," Marie responded.

The footpath ended where the lush swale grass began at the bog's edge, since the grass outgrew the wear on the seldom-used trail. But Marie pointed confidently to a gap in the trees on the far side of the bog. "We'll just keep our eyes on that openin' in the woods an' we'll make a straight line. Eagle Lake's just across the next ridge."

"How'll we cross the bog stream?" Maggie inquired, noting the narrow, but deep brook that flowed into Allagash Lake just to the south, on their right hand.

"Log bridge. All these trails have log bridges. Be no point in a trail if there weren't no bridge, *non*?"

But there was no bridge. And when the girls tried to find their way back to the trail, west of them on high ground, with no sun out to give them direction, nor mossy trees in their vast sea of swale grass to determine which way was north, they quickly became confused. So they could only head for high ground, keep the lake on their left, and blunder on.

Grandpa was right, Maggie fumed to herself as they walked. *Grandpa is always right!*

Maggie and Marie straggled with muddy shoes and rumpled dresses into Eagle Lake Camp just before Thanksgiving dinner was served that evening, only to find that the old-timers' chopping contest was long over. Grandpa had beaten men from both the Allagash Wilderness and Penobscot River regions in the first two rounds. But he had lost, by two or three strokes of his axe, a final contest with the champion old-timer of the St. John River Valley, known as *Le Roi du* St. John— The King. He was a man twenty years younger than Grandpa and two inches taller.

🦃 🦃 🦃

Maggie paddled without complaining next morning as she and Grandpa pushed westward across Eagle, Chamberlain, and Allagash Lakes toward The Elms. There was no tugboat to shorten their journey this day, for the logging crew had taken an extra day off to relax and make merry at the camp.

But Maggie fretted within herself, angry at herself for letting Marie talk her into trying a "shortcut," angry at Marie for convincing her to ignore Grandpa's penciled map. A knot tightened in her stomach as she realized that had they followed the map, she would have been there in time to see Grandpa win the second chopping contest.

The sun grew hot, and Maggie peeled off Father's blue wool Union Army jacket, then paddled all the harder. She paused only once again—to push her heavy, hot military cap to the back of her head.

By noon, Maggie and Grandpa were beaching their canoe at The Elms. Jake met them, grinning. "That mare, she's had twins—two colts," he called as Grandpa and Maggie climbed out of their canoe. "Mother and children, they are healthy," he said.

❦ ❦ ❦

"My old bones are still achin' from all that choppin'," Grandpa grumbled next morning as he was pouring their fresh Jersey milk through cheesecloth to strain it.

"But you practiced for nearly two weeks to get in shape, Grandpa."

"Sure enough," the old man agreed. "But when you're tryin' t' beat another chopper, you work that much harder." He said no more about his aches and pains, and after breakfast he returned to the barn to tend the horses, as usual.

As soon as Maggie had done the breakfast dishes, she spread her books out on the kitchen table by the window toward the horse pastures and fields. She couldn't get into her work, somehow. She gazed across the fields, where the elms and maples now stood bare of leaves against the pale fall sky. A crow, evidently searching for a missed ear of corn among the few stalks left in the garden, caught Maggie's eye. With a caw it suddenly flapped off for the forest, Bowser yipping after it in pursuit.

If only Marie were here, Maggie mused. *I'd not be angry with her now, and we could study together.* Yet Maggie *was* angry. It would be two days yet before Marie would come to study with her, and Maggie was not certain if she wanted to see Marie or not.

❦ ❦ ❦

Next morning Maggie found the stove cold when she came to the kitchen to prepare breakfast. Grumbling about Grandpa's thoughtlessness, she built the fire. But by the time the pancakes were ready, the teapot hot, and the table set, Grandpa had not come in from the barn.

So Maggie lit her small lamp and trotted through the long sheds to Molly's lonely stall next to where the hens had their own room. Molly mooed expectantly as Maggie approached. Grandpa was not to be seen!

Up the back stairs Maggie ran and hurried through her room. She opened the door to the main hall. "Grandpa!" No answer.

Quickly Maggie ran to Grandpa's room. "Grandpa?"

Grandpa moaned.

Maggie hurried to his bedside, anxious with fear. "Grandpa?"

"Oh, I ache all over, an' I'm cold."

Maggie found a blanket in his cedar chest and added it to the one already on the bed. She built a fire in the small stove. She then made Grandpa tea, but he took only a few sips.

"G-g-get Jake t' feed the horses," he groaned after a while. "I'll be all right till you get back."

Jake, of course, went straight to Grandpa's bedroom as soon as Maggie brought him back to The Elms. Long he sat with Grandpa, peering at him, speaking to him softly. "Bill Fuller, he very sick man," Jake said at last, rising from his chair. "You watch him. I go feed the horses."

"What do you think's wrong, Jake?" Maggie pleaded, as Jake shuffled toward the door.

"Jake not know. Maybe his old heart. The doctor, he would know. But Bill, he too old for the chopping contest, *non*?"

Grandpa did not improve during the next day, but he did not seem to be worse, either. He would eat nothing, and he drank only tea. Several times he threw up. Once Jake helped him into a chair where he sat wrapped in a blanket beside the bed so Maggie could change his sheets, soaked with perspiration.

Maggie had tried desperately several times to get the attention of the tugboat's crew, hoping they could send a message to Doctor Ross, the traveling physician who made the rounds of the logging camps. The men, however, had not heard her cries. Then, the third day of Grandpa's illness, Maggie heard soft steps in the hall. The door opened. "How is the patient?" It was Marie.

"Marie! Quick! I've gotta stop the tug before it gets away." Maggie raced off, but she returned soon in tears. The boat had left, and the men had not heard her frantic yells.

"*Grand-père*, he's been very sick, Jake tell me in the barn. But not to worry, he's better now. See how well he sleeps." She pointed toward Grandpa Fuller, who lay snoring heavily.

"But . . . but how can you say he's better?" Maggie whispered.

"No more fever. Cool as an otter on ice," Marie said confidently, placing her hand on the old man's brow. "Jake say he's been sweating an' throwing up, *non*?"

"Yes," Maggie said, "that's true."

"*La grippe*—the flu, you *Anglais* call it. It's all over Eagle Lake Camp. *Grand-père*, he caught it there, for sure. *Maman*, she is the camp nurse as well as the cook, and she teach me these things. Patients with *la grippe* always get better, with rest, *Maman* says. But *Grand-père*, he is old, so he need more rest than most," she said solemnly. "Give him two, maybe three days an' he be feeding the horses again. Then Jake can go home."

Forgotten now was Maggie's anger toward Marie for leading her down a dead-end trail to the bog. Forgotten, too, was her own shame at having allowed headstrong Marie to talk her into ignoring Grandpa's instructions to follow the map and stay on the trail he had marked. Grandpa was on the mend, and that was all that mattered to Maggie now.

Chapter 9

A Difference in Values

Grandpa Fuller was better next morning, as Marie had predicted. He was well enough, in fact, to get dressed, to put on an extra wool shirt and slippers, and shuffle to the barn to check on the new twin colts and see how well Jake was doing tending the livestock.

"Bill Fuller," Jake advised him, "the horses is okay, *non*? I milk the cow an' get all the stalls clean. Now you get in house an' sit by the stove 'fore you catch 'monia."

Grandpa knew, of course, that old folks, weakened by a bout with the flu, sometimes catch pneumonia and die if they don't get proper rest. So, though it bothered him to take orders from Jake, he returned to the warm kitchen, where Maggie and Marie had been taking turns baking cookies in the wood stove's hot oven between sessions of working out exercises in *Harvey's Grammar*.

"Molasses cookie, Grandpa?" Maggie asked brightly. "It's Grandma's recipe. I even found her old rolling pin to roll 'em out with."

"Don't mind if I do. The walk to the barn sure gave me an appetite."

"There's a batch in the oven right now. Be ready in

five minutes. Would you like tea to go with 'em or coffee? Teakettle's hot."

"Make it coffee. I've drunk so much tea in the past two days I'm beginning to talk with a British accent." He tossed his heavy shirt on the back of his rocking chair and went into the sitting room, where Jake had slept on the davenport for the past two nights.

"Phew!" Grandpa said moments later, as he returned to the kitchen and closed the door after him. "That room smells like a whole den full of skunks, an' it looks like the Battle of Bull Run was fought in there. I guess I'm lucky Jake always knew when we were comin' home so's he could tidy things up an' air the house out when I've left him here alone," he said with a sigh as he collapsed into his rocker.

The room was silent for some moments except for the diligent scratching of Marie's pencil at the table and the clang and squeak of the heavy iron oven door as Maggie took out a fresh batch of cookies and put in another. "I wish that old bathtub didn't leak," Grandpa grumbled at last. "I'd show Jake how t' use it."

"Coffee, Grandpa?" Maggie quickly interrupted, thrusting his mustache cup into his hand. "Say when," she said, bringing the agate coffeepot menacingly close to his face.

"Sure." Grandpa sat up from his slouch and held the cup for Maggie to pour. Doing so, he caught sight of Jake, who had padded into the kitchen in his high-top moosehide moccasins just as Grandpa had begun his tirade about Jake's needing a bath.

"Bill, he needn't worry. Jake be out of here tomorrow, Indian smell an' all," Jake remarked. "Jake take a bath, come spring when lake warm up," he added, stepping into the sitting room and closing the door after him.

"Guess your old grandpa put his foot in his mouth that time," Grandpa muttered between sips of coffee and bites of molasses cookie.

"Have another cookie?" Maggie asked.

"No. No thanks." He thrust out his cup, still half-full. "Here. I'm goin' upstairs to nap for an hour or two." Grandpa rose and shuffled toward the hall door.

As soon as Maggie had taken the last batch of cookies from the oven, she hurried to the foot of the front stairs. Upstairs she could hear Grandpa vigorously shaking down the ashes in his small bedroom stove. Satisfied that Grandpa was all right, Maggie returned to the kitchen. "Let's go outdoors," she told Marie at once.

"Good idea. Where to?"

"I'd like to paddle down the lake in Grandpa's canoe—just to get away from here!"

"Marie, she get all the paddling she need going back an' forth from Eagle Lake Camp. But if you want a ride on the lake, we go, Maggie." Marie's tone showed both disappointment and forced enthusiasm. Ordinarily Maggie would have suggested they do something else. But this morning, with Grandpa mad at himself and Jake mad at Grandpa, she was determined to get away fast.

"Like you, I'm tired of tending sick men an' feeding smelly trappers," Marie remarked as the girls pushed the canoe into the lake.

"I can't stand men—any men!"

"So, *Grand-père*? You not stand him, either, I guess?"

"Grandpa's different—he's not—" Maggie almost said, "Grandpa's not a man," but she stopped herself. "Well, Grandpa's different, that's all."

"*Grand-père* is not what?" Marie queried. "Not really a man, maybe. Like my *maman* is not a woman, 'cause she's just *Maman* to me. But the men at Eagle Lake Camp, they see her different. They see a woman, Evangeline LaRochelle, when they look at her, and a pretty one she is, too."

"So what are you trying to say about Grandpa?" Maggie wanted to know.

"Only that Bill Fuller is a *grand-père* to you, and *grand-pères* are always kind and good, *non*? But to Jake, Bill is a man, an' men make mistakes, sometimes they get angry, say mean things, mebbe even act like children."

"So do women," Maggie defended.

"Of course. That's my point. That's what I mean about *Maman*. She is kind to me, like the mother she is. But to others she is Evangeline the cook, a woman."

The truth that Marie was trying to point out was beginning to dawn on Maggie. "So I guess I've believed that Grandpa was always right, and when others disagreed with him, they were always wrong." She sighed. "But I guess that's not always the truth."

The lake, though dark, was smooth as polished pewter as the girls pushed their canoe across its surface. Above them, the fall sky spread steel gray, no hint of the summer sun showing through. Even though Maggie was working hard at her paddle, she kept her father's old army coat pulled close against the icy fingers of an early winter.

"Oh-o-o-o-o-o-o-o, ow, ow, ow, oh-h-h-h-o-o-oo!"

Maggie had heard that cry before, and it always gave her the shivers. She turned in the direction of the unearthly scream and spied a feathered, coal-black, seemingly disembodied head with a heavy black beak. The creature watched them with beady eyes as it rested on the dark surface of the water. The bird then dived, its great black webbed feet flying behind as it disappeared.

"The great northern diver, the loon!" exclaimed Marie. "An' it's going to come up right in our path. Let's get closer."

The girls bent to their paddles, and the canoe shot ahead. Maggie had often seen loons in her weeks at The Elms. They had always been far, far out on the lake, usually appearing only at dawn before the waters of the lake were disturbed by daytime breezes or at dusk after the steam tugboat had left for Chamberlain Lake. She would watch their antics from the verandah as they gave out their doleful wails, then dived for fish, to reappear hundreds of feet away.

Suddenly there it was, and both girls stopped paddling at once to view this magnificent bird, floating on its white belly on the water's surface, a wriggling trout dangling from its black beak. The loon had a long neck ringed in black like an undertaker's bow tie. Its black back was checkered in white, and its breast, though partly under water, was silvery white. As their canoe glided closer, the fishing bird dived, not to be seen again that day.

"I guess I just don't understand men," Maggie said, trying to wrest from Marie more of her interesting point of view about men and boys.

"What's to understand? I'd just like to see one once in a while," Marie commented.

"One? There must be two hundred at Eagle Lake Camp. Tall ones, short ones, skinny ones, and ones with muscles," Maggie chuckled.

"Boys my own age, I mean. You know, Maggie, I've never, ever in my whole life even talked with a boy my own age—or even close. None of the men at Eagle are under seventeen. *Maman* has nephews in Quebec City, but they're all little kids. I'd give anything for a brother."

"I've got a stepbrother you can have," Maggie put in.

"You're lucky! What's wrong with him?"

"Why would there be anything wrong with Jacky?" Maggie pretended to be offended.

"*Maman* always said to pick a guy on the basis of his worst faults because you're goin' to have to live with them. They won't change," Marie explained.

"Jacky hates dogs, for openers. And I think he's stuck-up. He grew up in the city."

"Oh, ho!" Marie had caught Maggie off guard, and Maggie was soon to hurt for it. "So the pot calls the kettle black! So *Grand-père* stick his foot in his mouth, but Maggie, she stick both feet in, city shoes an' all. So it's 'love me, love my dog' for the girl who's afraid of Indians an' who doesn't like us dirty Frenchies!"

"You mean 'love me, love my frog,'" Maggie quickly answered, turning Marie's scolding into a joke.

"Toad," Marie corrected. Both girls doubled over in such convulsive laughter that they had to drop their paddles and let the canoe drift.

❧ ❧ ❧

The little group in the big house spent an uneasy

evening that night. Maggie and Marie played checkers in the light of the lamp at the kitchen table, while Grandpa Fuller, his rocking chair back toward the lamp to let the light fall over his shoulder, read his Bible, chapter after chapter, all evening.

Jake Beavertail sat across the room in the shadows by the grate of the stove, smoking his pipe and paring and slicing northern spy apples to eat with his near-toothless gums. From time to time Jake would stir, only to put another junk of rock maple in the cook-stove's small firebox or knock the ashes from his pipe through the glowing grate.

Once, when Jake rose and trod toward the wood-shed in the ell, Maggie's game was disturbed by the bang of the door behind him. "Oh, my," she said. "I forgot to fill the woodbox today, and it's my job." She rose and started after Jake.

"Don't," Grandpa quietly advised, holding up his hand. "Jake's been extra helpful today. I think he's trying to make a point."

The tall clock in the hall struck nine, its bell ringing the deep, haunting bass notes that caused Maggie to crawl deeper into her feather bed when she heard it strike in the night. Grandpa placed his Bible on the table and folded his reading glasses, placing them on the Bible.

"Is that a Bible you've been readin', *Grand-père* Fuller?" Marie inquired. "My *maman* reads the Bible, too, only hers is French," she added without waiting for Grandpa to answer her. "I wish *Maman* would read the Bible to me sometime—or teach me to read it for myself. The priest reads the Bible in church. It is God's Word, *non*?"

"My mother used to read her Bible to me," Grandpa said, his voice tired and old sounding. "That was long, long ago." After a pause he added, "It's bedtime for folks who have to get up in the morning."

Next morning before dawn, when Maggie and Marie came downstairs to fix breakfast, a fire crackled in the stove and the spider sat on the back of the stove where it had been pushed aside after someone had fried eggs and potatoes. The sitting room door was open, so Maggie peered inside. Every cushion was in place on the sofa, and Jake's wicker knapsack was gone.

Maggie checked the coathooks beside the door to the ell. Grandpa's denim chore frock was gone. So was Jake's deerskin coat. "Marie can . . . can you start breakfast? I've gotta talk with Grandpa."

"Sure. Just let me get the lamp lit 'fore you go off with your lamp."

Maggie found Grandpa in the barn on his three-legged stool, milking Molly. "Jake's gone, isn't he, Grandpa?"

"'Fraid so. Left early. He fixed his own breakfast an' slipped out 'fore I came downstairs."

"I . . . I hope Jake's not sore at us. Think he'll be back?"

"'Course he'll be back. We're still friends—I hope."

Somehow, Grandpa sounds defensive and worried, Maggie thought.

Chapter 10

Christmas in the Allagash

The lumber camps closed for a week at Christmas, and the French loggers returned to their villages and farms in Quebec for the long holiday. For three days men in stocking caps, plaid mackinaws, and red suspenders streamed out of the woods or across the frozen lake to bring their horses to The Elms' great horse barn for Grandpa to tend while they were away.

"I want to spend Christmas right here, with you, Grandpa," Maggie said firmly one day a week before Christmas. Grandpa and Maggie had been talking about the best way for her to make the long trek back to Laketon so she could be with Mama at Christmas. "I can't bear to leave you alone. Mama has her own family with her," Maggie told him. "Why does she need me?"

Deep inside, Maggie knew, too, that her anger toward Jacky still burned. Maggie's friendship with Marie had brought some of this bitterness toward Jacky to the surface, and she did not like to be reminded of it.

"Jake'll be here," Grandpa said, "so I won't be alone."

"I know," Maggie said sadly. She remembered American Thanksgiving Day, only weeks earlier in

late November, when Jake had dropped by to share
their turkey and pies. Jake had not been around The
Elms since that morning in October when he had
slipped off without saying good-bye. He was cordial
to Grandpa and as chivalrous as ever toward Maggie,
but he nevertheless seemed to be cool and distant,
Maggie thought.

Just three days before Christmas, North Woods
Logging Company's horseback riding courier made
his weekly visit to bring the mail from the world
outside. He brought Grandpa several Christmas cards,
one from a woman, Jeanne d'Arc Lalibertie, who Maggie had noticed had been writing Grandpa quite
frequently. And for Maggie he brought a letter, post-
marked Laketon.

Maggie pulled Grandpa's rocker up to the stove and
turned her back to the window to take full advantage
of the slanting rays of the December sun before she
tore open the envelope. She wished to savor every
syllable of her letter from home.

Dear Maggie,

John and I and Jacky have started going
to church. I missed church very much after
your father died, but I couldn't bring myself to attend weekly services, being a widow
and alone. Church is something you have
missed growing up, except for holidays
and summer Bible classes, I'm afraid.

Now that we are a family again, I very
much want us all together at Christmas.
So John was able to get a few days off,
and we've borrowed a pair of horses and a

two-seat sleigh for the trip. We'll take a freight train as far as the sawmill, and the horses can ride free in an empty boxcar. We will all get to ride in the caboose, since there are no passenger cars, which is fine with me, but Jacky, who is still pretty much a city boy, thinks it's rather primitive.

Please tell your grandfather if it won't work out for us to come for a week over Christmas to let us know at once, so we can cancel our plans. We do expect to arrive on Christmas Eve in time for John and Jacky to cut a Christmas tree, if your grandfather hasn't got one already. I shall bring a box of trimmings.

Love,

Mother

P.S. Grandma Ridlon is taking the stage-coach to Foxcroft to spend Christmas with her sister, Aunt Minnie.

There was a note from Jacky, written on the same paper, after Mama's.

Dear Maggie,

School is going well, and I've actually made some friends in this small "one-horse town," though some of the kids are real hicks. One boy smells so much like a cow barn that I'm surprised he doesn't bring his cows to school. I'm used to a much larger school, but they seem to have all the subjects here, so I guess I'll be ready for academy when I graduate from grammar school, anyway.

See you at Christmas.

Your brother,

Jack Hanscombe

"Katy must think that we have daily U.S. Mail service up here in the woods," Grandpa chuckled after reading Mother's letter. "But no matter—we've got the room, that's for sure.

"Let's see," Grandpa continued, thinking out loud, "I can put Jake in the girl's room that was to have been yours, but you chose the maid's quarters instead. He'll really get a charge out o' that—pink walls 'n' such. Jake sure likes bright colors. We'll need the sittin' room for the tree an' visitin'.

"Katy an' John'll get the guest room. That leaves Jacky. He can have that nice boy's room in the attic, on the third floor at the head o' the stairs."

Maggie's schoolbooks were forgotten as she spent the next three days dusting, mopping floors, and knocking down cobwebs from corners in bedrooms that hadn't been tidied up since Grandma Fuller had died years ago. She found clean sheets and blankets enough for all the beds, and at Grandpa's suggestion, Maggie spread the musty-smelling sheets loosely over the beds to let them air out for a day before making the beds up with Grandma's old handmade quilts. "They can't expect hotel service here," Grandpa said when he saw how hard Maggie was working, "but at least we'll do our best."

"How're we going to heat all those extra bedrooms, Grandpa?" Maggie asked on the middle of the second day of sweeping floors, wiping varnished woodwork with cedar oil, beating carpets, and making beds. She had worn a sweater under Father's sergeant's coat during most of her work, and still she was cold, working in winter in those unheated rooms.

Grandpa scratched his bald head. "Let's see. There's maybe a ton o' coal under the firewood in the shed, left from when the company president lived here. I've never cared for the smell o' coal, but it sure beats tryin' t' tote enough firewood upstairs several times a day t' keep the bedrooms warm. Tell you what. I can throw over enough firewood to expose a corner of that coal pile. Take me an hour or two diggin' through it. Then can you carry a bucketful up t' each bedroom—or are you tuckered out?"

"Well . . . ," Maggie hesitated. She knew Grandpa's arthritis wouldn't let him make that many trips upstairs, but she had other plans for the afternoon. Still, the house ought to be warm before the guests arrived. It wouldn't do to wait for John and Jacky Hanscombe to lug the coal. "Well, I had hoped to bake some apple pies. There are plenty of Northern Spies in the cellar, aren't there?"

"Sure are. Wolf Rivers, too—take your pick. But unless I miss my guess your ma will bring a basket of pies, frozen in transit an' ready to heat in the oven. But if you want to bake cookies, I'll help mix the dough after supper."

So Maggie carried the coal. She also carried fresh towels to every room and placed a new bar of soap on each bedside table, along with a porcelain pitcher of wash water. Then she thought better of it. *Suppose the water freezes and cracks the pitchers*, she worried. *There won't be any heat in the bedrooms until tomorrow.* Carrying each pitcher back to the bathroom, Maggie dumped the water out.

The thermometer by the back door had not risen above freezing since Thanksgiving, and it had dipped below zero every night for more than two weeks prior to Christmas. On the morning of Christmas Eve it read minus thirty-seven degrees when Maggie had let Bowser out for his run. Maggie was glad to see it so cold, even though it was a constant battle to keep Jack Frost outdoors. She knew there were many frozen brooks, streams, and lakes for Mama's family to cross on their sleigh where there would be no bridges.

Snow had been light that year—not more than six inches so far—just enough for easy sledding, yet not enough for heavy going. Jake arrived at noon the day before Christmas, wicker knapsack on his back, beaver-paw snowshoes of waxed leather thongs tied onto the knapsack.

"What are the snowshoes for, Jake?" Maggie asked. "There's not snow enough to need them."

"Maggie and Bill Fuller would have to put up with old Jake the rest of the winter if a blizzard struck and Jake not have snowshoes, *non*?"

Maggie sincerely wished she hadn't asked Jake to answer the obvious.

It was three o'clock in the afternoon on Christmas Eve, and the early December night of northern New England had already drawn the low, south-traveling sun near the western hills where soon it would dip from view, pulling the silver threads of mercury in the thermometers across Maine even lower as it dropped. As Maggie stepped onto the verandah to peer across the frozen lake toward the outlet stream for the dozenth time, at least, since noon, she saw that the shadow of the house, ell, and barn now stretched far across the snow-covered lake. Maggie peered far down the lake, and glistening puffs of light-reflecting water vapor shining in the brilliant rays of the slanting sun caught her eye. Four puffs of vapor there were, seeming to float and bounce several feet above the ice in the gathering darkness, appearing and disappearing, reappearing and disappearing in the regular rhythm of the heavy breathing of trotting horses. Maggie's ears picked up the "clink, clink, clink" of small brass bells jingling in time with the eerie, glowing vapor from the nostrils of two horses. Then she spied a moving mass coming up the lake behind the vapor in the direction of the tinkling. A large, black, double-seated sleigh drawn by two dapple-gray horses, its three passengers swaddled nearly out of sight in brown buffalo robes, began to take shape.

Maggie waited only long enough to make sure that the mass moving toward The Elms was indeed a team crossing the ice, then she ran inside: "Grandpa, they're coming! They're coming!" Maggie grabbed her coat and army cap and ran for the front door, Bowser bounding joyfully ahead. Then, remembering that the thermometer was still well below zero, she raced back for a scarf.

After a ten-minute walk along the ice, Maggie met the sleigh. "Whoa, whoa back, girls," John called to the mares as he tightened the reins. Maggie bounded aboard, and though Mama would have kissed her and sent her to sit in the backseat with Jacky, Maggie crowded between Katherine and John for the run across the last stretch of ice and the long climb up the grade to the house.

Grandpa Fuller met the happy family at the side entrance leading into the ell and the kitchen. He quickly shook hands with John and Jacky, then gave his daughter, Katy, a bone-crushing hug, followed by a kiss on the forehead.

The entire crowd, Jake included, pitched in to bundle packages, pies, and buffalo-hide robes into the house. "Got our Christmas tree yet, Papa?" Mama asked Grandpa.

"I've got a great one picked out, Katy," he replied. He pointed to a row of white birches beyond a rail fence at the far side of the pasture where a balsam fir stood out among them, green and stark, glistening in the setting sun. "If John and Jacky can hustle over there while I put your horses an' sleigh in the barn, they can cut it an' have it back 'fore it gets too dark t' see."

"C'mon, Pa," Jacky cried at once. Not waiting for Grandpa to get his axe from the woodshed, Jacky pulled out the hatchet John had brought in the sleigh for emergencies.

"We'll use that to prune our tree, perhaps," Pa explained. "Bill, where can we find an axe?" he asked Grandpa.

Jacky Hanscombe may have been a city boy with a dislike for "hicks" and farm boys, but lazy he was not when the occasion demanded action. By the time Mama and Maggie had piled the Christmas packages in the sitting room and sent the pies to the cellar on the dumbwaiter, Jacky was on the verandah, knocking the snow off the Christmas tree he had helped Pa Hanscombe cut. "Hold your horses," hollered Grandpa from the sitting room. "John, come help me 'n' Jake drag this straw matting into the hall. Fancy thing'll be so full o' fir needles I'll never get it clean, if we set the tree on it."

❦ ❦ ❦

No holiday dinner was ever served like the one Maggie's family ate that Christmas Day at The Elms. Two Canada geese, which Grandpa had shot earlier and hung to freeze under the rafters of the frigid woodshed, went into the oven long before dawn.

"Jacky, there's a big blue squash in the cellar," Grandpa declared as soon as breakfast was done. "It's a huge one; you'll find it over by the cistern. See if you can rassle it up the stairs to the woodshed an' bust it up on the choppin' block. Feed the seeds to the chickens. Then I'll help you pare it with my jack-knife."

Jacky disappeared through the door to the ell, and Grandpa, Jake, and John took their coats and went in the same direction to feed the horses.

"Bump, thump, ugh! Bump, thump, ugh! Bump— boom! Boom! Rumble, rumble, rumble!"

"Ma!"

Mama and Maggie rushed to the cellar stairs. There sat Jacky, nearly to the top, a look of great disgust on his face.

"What happened, for heaven's sake?" Mother inquired.

"Ma, I've never seen such a squash. That thing weighs a ton!"

"Well, I declare, it certainly looks more like a whale or an elephant than a vegetable," Mama said, peering down the long stairs at the hubbard squash, which lay on the bedrock cellar floor. "Go get your pa an' have him tote it to the choppin' block for you."

John Hanscombe carried the huge squash up the cellar stairs, and Mama and Maggie stepped again into the back entry to admire the fruit of Grandpa's garden, as John sat on it, panting. "I've sent Jacky for Bill's wheelbarrow," John explained. "I'm taking this fellow to the barn an' weigh it on the grain scales."

"If Grandpa raised buttercup squash, we could have split 'em with the meat cleaver," observed Maggie.

"Your grandfather never was one to be *practical*," put in Mama. "To him, if it's bigger, it's better. When I was your age he shot a moose, then had to hire a neighbor with a team of oxen to drag it out of the woods. He must've passed up a dozen deer he could've dragged home alone. But not Bill Fuller—no sir! He had to have the biggest animal in the woods, even if it took Grandma Fuller and me three days to cut it up, and three more days toting the meat we couldn't eat around to the neighbors."

John weighed the hubbard. "Eighty-three pounds and five ounces," he declared. "Bigger'n the all-time blue ribbon grand champion at Foxcroft State Fair by twenty pounds, at least."

Fortunately for Maggie and Mama, after Jacky split the squash with Grandpa's axe, John good-naturedly spent an hour and a half in the sitting room helping Jacky and Grandpa pare the squash, which they then set to boil on the sitting room heating stove. Not only was this monster vegetable sufficient for Christmas dinner, and several more meals during the week to follow, but Mother packed the remainder into two large earthenware mixing bowls, covered them with cloth, and set them in the woodshed to freeze for Maggie and Grandpa to eat during the winter months.

John declared the goose gravy to be "Better'n they serve in the best hotel restaurants in Boston." No one doubted his word, for he was the only one present who'd ever been to Boston.

Jake brought cranberries he had picked on a marsh next to the lake in October and then stored in his cellar. Mama boiled the berries, drained the juice into a crock, added a gallon of hot tea, brewed fresh with cinnamon sticks and whole cloves, then stirred in a pint of honey while it was still hot. She set the crock into the snow on the verandah to chill, and the family had punch enough for the next several days.

Maggie, alone in her chamber above the kitchen that night, slept fitfully at first. She was torn between wanting to return to Laketon and home with Mama and John and Jacky and her determination to winter in the wilderness at The Elms with Grandpa. Maggie tossed and turned, considering her options. Still, Mama's family would be houseguests at The Elms for another week, until after New Year's Day, so she need not decide that evening.

Bowser, curled up on the warm register in Maggie's room above the kitchen stove, finally found that the cast-iron grate had grown cold under him, since the fire had gone out in the range. The hound hopped onto the bed some moments after the tall clock's gong had sounded the midnight hour. He curled himself up on her feet, and dog and mistress slept soundly until morning.

Chapter 11

Brother and Sister

The week after Christmas passed with Maggie and Jacky entertaining each other in a more-or-less cordial truce. Mother and John had brought Maggie a new, six-foot toboggan. It had been strapped across the back of the sleigh for the trip from Laketon, so it was hardly a surprise on Christmas morning.

"The toboggan, she needs wax to slide better," Jake observed after watching the young people take several trips down the long grade from the end of the barn, sailing past the house and onto the frozen lake. The toboggan glided along well enough, it seemed to Jacky and Maggie, who were riding tandem and taking turns steering for the downhill run. But no sooner did they reach the flat, snow-covered lake surface, than the toboggan began to lose momentum rapidly, then stopped not far from shore.

So Jacky trudged with the toboggan back to the house. He held it upright on the verandah while Maggie vigorously worked it over with a kitchen broom, getting off most of the snow now sticking in large patches on its undersurface.

"We don't have room for that thing in the kitchen," fussed Mama, as her child and stepchild dragged the

toboggan inside, intending to warm its wooden surface beside the hot kitchen range. "It'll drip all over
the floor."

"Take it into the sittin' room, an' prop it on a chair
beside the stove," Grandpa interrupted. "I've got a
can of beeswax in my workshop. Jake can show you
how to wax it, soon's the toboggan's dried out and
warmed through."

🍂 🍂 🍂

Far, far out on the ice the toboggan now shot—so
far, in fact, that after three or four fast downhill trips,
Jacky tired of trudging back to the barn through the
ankle-deep snow. "It's getting late. I want to go to the
barn and help Pa and Grandpa feed the horses," Jacky
growled.

"Three more runs," responded Maggie, who had
seen workhorses every day since coming to The Elms
and often helped feed them hay, oats, and water. Now
that the barn was full of horses, however, Maggie had
walked behind the horse stalls only once—that was
enough. The huge creatures, much larger than saddle
horses, towered far above her head, and their heavy,
steel-shod hooves looked as though they could crush
her like an ant, should one of them carelessly step
toward her. She was not about to admit her nervous-
ness to Jacky, for she knew that though he was unused
to large horses such as these, he bravely walked behind them with the men, even helping clean the stalls.
Jacky was one big contradiction to Maggie. Though he
had complained to her that The Elms' barn "stinks like
the town dump," he seemed to consider it masculine
to work there with the men.

"Ahh, I'm tired of this game," Jacky answered. "I'll slide some more tomorrow. Besides, you can slide better without me."

"We're just getting started," protested Maggie, who to tell the truth, found sliding with Jacky fun.

"All right," Jacky gave in, "one more trip." Together brother and sister trudged up to the barn. Jacky lay flat on the toboggan and grabbed the rope to steer. Maggie piled on top, and they were off. Jacky steered close to the roots of a huge, gnarled yellow birch, where the embankment leading down to the beach was steeper than the gradual slope by the boat launch where they had been sliding. The toboggan bounced high, then plummeted down and sailed across the snow-covered ice with Jacky aboard.

Maggie, however, found herself headfirst in a snowdrift just under the embankment. Her collar was full of snow that trickled beneath her sweater and dress. Her mittens were full, and snow went up her sleeves to her elbows.

By the time Jacky got back to high ground, Maggie had shaken the snow out of her clothes, ready for another run. Jacky, seeing his stepsister's embarrassment, grinned at her and inwardly considered taking another run with her to make up for the nasty spill.

"You did that on purpose, Jacky Hanscombe," Maggie snapped.

"Sure I did," Jacky admitted. "That shallow slope was boring. This is fun!"

"You didn't have to dump me!"

"Dump you? If you'd 'a' hung on to the side ropes 'stead o' huggin' me, you wouldn't have got thrown."

"C'mon," Maggie demanded, "let's take another run. I'll steer this time."

"Suit yourself—take all the trips you want. I'm goin' to the barn." Jacky tossed Maggie the tow rope and strode off.

"Where's Jacky?" Mama inquired pleasantly moments later, as Maggie slogged into the kitchen without bothering to brush the snow off her leggings and shoes.

"Out'n the barn with the men," Maggie answered in a tone that caused Mama to change her mind about scolding her for being so careless. Maggie trudged upstairs to her room where she peeled off her outer clothes and hung them on a folding wooden clotheshorse over the register to dry. Pulling a quilt over her slip and bloomers, Maggie curled up in an old platform rocker by her window and read *Great Expectations* until the sun slipped beyond the pines at the edge of the pasture and she could no longer see the words on the pages.

"I guess Jake had the answer to your sliding problem," chuckled Grandpa to Maggie and Jacky, as he and Jake sat chatting beside the sitting room stove that evening.

"Ol' Jake, he know a few tricks of the woods," Jake remarked to the brother and sister. "I have a small toboggan of my own that I keep waxed like my snowshoes. The city folk, they come here from Foxcroft or Quebec to go hunting. They struggle through the woods durin' huntin' season with sleds that drag like pullin' on dirt," he chortled.

Maggie and Jacky were playing checkers together while lying on their stomachs under the Christmas tree. Since they were both still sore at each other about the spill under the yellow birch's roots, they ignored Grandpa and Jake's pleasant comments.

"Maybe you get the beeswax too thin, *non*?" Jake inquired. Seeing that he was not getting an answer, Jake finally let the matter drop.

❦ ❦ ❦

New Year's Day the family had another holiday meal, a venison roast from a fat buck Grandpa had shot as it was raiding his corn patch in late fall. Mama baked potatoes, and with leftover goose gravy kept frozen in the woodshed, the family ate very well, indeed.

"Too bad Jake had to leave," Mama murmured. "He'd sure enjoy this deer meat roast."

"Jake left 'cause he doesn't like crowds," Grandpa replied. "By noon tomorrow this place'll be crawlin' with woodcutters after their horses."

"Can we stay an' see the *real* lumberjacks, Pa?" cried Jacky.

"I'm sorry, son," John replied. "We're pullin' out o' here right after breakfast. Our team's really got to trot if we're going to catch the train at the sawmill by one o'clock."

"*Lumberjacks*," Maggie mimicked Jacky. "Still a *city boy*. Nobody calls 'em lumberjacks 'cept in storybooks—an' city people."

After midnight that night Maggie heard the hall door to her chamber over the kitchen open. The steps leading down into her room creaked. "Maggie?" a voice whispered.

Maggie struck a match for light before answering. Jacky stood at the door to the steps in flannel pajamas and a wool bathrobe. "What do you want?" she asked.

"There's this weird noise, like someone with a sore throat screaming for help. I think it's on the roof."

"That's silly. Go back to bed."

"I mean it. I can't sleep with that racket goin' on."

"Oh, all right." Maggie struck another match and lit her bedside lamp. She slid her feet over the edge of the bed and into her felt slippers. Standing up, she grabbed Father's army jacket and slipped it over her nightgown. "Sergeant Maggie to the rescue," she yawned. As a final touch, Maggie clapped her Union Army infantryman's cap over her red hair. "C'mon," she said, picking up her lamp.

Rounding her bed, Maggie paused at the window to look out. The full moon illuminated the landscape, and here and there a cloud floated across the sky. A light snow of perhaps an inch had fallen during the day. Maggie watched as the night wind picked up the light, white crystals by the bushel and whirled them in eerie spirals across fields and lake. It had been calm when Maggie went to bed, but the wind now shook the tall house and made its heavy timbers groan.

Maggie loved nights like this. Snug in flannel between comforter and featherbed, she could pretend to be secure in the midst of a wild storm, God watching over her. The only occasion that gave her more pleasure was August thundershowers at night, when claps of thunder rattled the windowpanes as bolts of lightning illuminated her room.

Maggie led the way up the three steps and down the long hall to where a door led to the attic stairs and Jacky's bedroom above. She turned the wooden button, opened the door, and was about to climb the stairs. "There 'tis," Jacky whispered suddenly.

Maggie had heard that noise during storms before but not as distinctly, and she had never bothered to investigate. *Old houses make strange sounds in storms*, she had always told herself. *Nothing to worry about.*

Maggie waited a moment, holding the lamp up to light the stairs. A low moan, followed by a raspy scream came distinctly from the attic. Another scream, another moan, a series of raw coughing noises, a long moan. Though she'd heard those same noises in the distance every windy night all fall and winter, up close they now gave her the shivers. Jacky was right— it *was* weird.

Maggie set her lip and ascended the stairs. A loud squawk from a loose stair tread beneath her foot stopped her halfway up. *Silly*, she told herself, fighting her fright, *it's only a loose board. The noise in the attic has a logical explanation, too.*

The sounds led Maggie and Jacky into an open, unfinished attic storage room next to his bedroom. Maggie had been there before, in August, when she had helped Grandpa move the boxes stored in her bedroom to the attic. She raised the lamp high, and the light gleamed from the tips of shingle nails protruding through the roof's underside, white with frost.

The moans and screams began again, Maggie noticed, only when the wind picked up. She placed her hand on the huge chimney that separated this unfinished room from Jacky's bedroom. The bricks were bare, though on the bedroom side they had been plastered over.

The scream came again. "It's coming from the chimney," Maggie whispered. "Put your hand up here, next to mine."

Jacky touched the bricks.

"Feel it? Feel the vibration?" Maggie asked, as the groan came loud, clear, and long.

"Yeah."

"Makes your fingers tingle, doesn't it?"

"Yeah. Is someone trapped in there?"

"You're too late for Santa Claus," Maggie chortled. "'Sides, if anyone was in there, they'd be smoked as a side of bacon by now, with all the stoves in the house goin' night an' day."

"Just the same, it makes me nervous." Jacky knew, of course, that nobody could possibly be in the chimney. But he also knew that he was scared at the strange screams, though he wasn't about to admit this to Maggie.

"Oh, cut it out," Maggie answered impatiently.

"Well, I'm sleepin' downstairs. Too noisy up here."

"Don't be silly, Jacky."

"I'll get my blanket an' sleep on the sofa in the sittin' room." He opened the door to his room.

"Don't bother," Maggie said hotly. "I'm sleepin' in your bed tonight. You can have mine." She went into his room with the lamp and left Jacky to feel his way back to her bedroom in the dark.

Jacky's room was cold that night, since his fire was nearly out. Maggie was used to getting her heat from her floor register, so she did not get up to stoke the stove. Sleepily she struggled to keep warm beneath the blanket.

Chapter 12

Maggie's Decision

———————

Next morning when Maggie slipped into her room to get her clothes, she found Bowser curled up on Jacky's feet. "I'm beginning to like this silly ol' hound," Jacky said, propping himself on one elbow and pulling Bowser by his collar until he was hugging the animal. "He's a nice doggie, fleas and all, now he's got over his puppy chewing stage."

Without answering, Maggie slipped down to the sitting room to dress by the stove. She was not at all certain that she wanted Jacky to like Bowser. Bowser was *her* hound.

At breakfast Maggie merrily told how Jacky had left his room because he was nervous about the noise in the chimney.

"That's the shanty cap," said Grandpa. "It squeaks an' groans in the wind somethin' wicked."

"A what?" Jacky asked.

"A shanty cap's a metal wind deflector that always turns away from the wind to make the stoves draw better on a windy night. Once it gets rusty, it'll squeak forever," Grandpa explained.

"Jacky was so scared he had to sleep in my bed," Maggie giggled. "He wouldn't stay upstairs."

"I tried to get back into my own bed, but Maggie leaped in ahead of me," Jacky tried to defend himself.

Maggie just glared at him.

After breakfast Maggie would not let Mama help with the dishes, knowing that she, John, and Jacky faced a long sleigh ride down the frozen lake and along an iced-over stream. Then they must travel several miles of rutted forest logging roads to reach the train at the sawmill in time to load the horses for a one o'clock departure for Laketon.

And Maggie had not admitted to Mama that she *wanted* Mama to hurry off before Maggie herself decided to grab her things and climb into the sleigh with them. She had not allowed herself to think about this, though deep within she wanted to go home.

No sooner had her parents left, than the loggers began to arrive for their horses. Brought to The Elms in large, heavy sleighs pulled by coach horses, two dozen logging company teamsters spent the next couple of hours harnessing their huge gray Percherons and brown Belgians. Hitching them to heavy, steel-runnered pungs—sleds used to tote logs through the frozen forest—they prepared for their day-long walk to the logging camps of the Allagash Wilderness.

After Maggie was done with the dishes, she slipped on her coat and army cap and strolled out to watch the men harness the horses. The loggers smoked pipes and chatted among themselves in French, though most of the men carefully knocked the lit tobacco into the snow before entering the barn, Maggie noticed. Their horses, she soon discovered, were called *chevaux*, and Grandpa's barn, actually a large horse stable, the men called *l'écurie*.

Then she discovered that Grandpa, ordinarily a mild-mannered man, knew a few French words and phrases himself. Two muscular young men in plaid wool coats so tattered there were patches on their patches were harnessing a pair of frisky stallions at one end of the barn's floor. One of these fellows was smoking a pipe inside the barn as he walked around his horses in the straw scattered on the floor, tightening a harness strap here, fastening a buckle there.

"*La pipe*," Grandpa said to him quietly, stepping up to the youth rather quickly and pointing to his lit pipe, "put it out *s'il vous plaît. Vous brûlerez l'écurie*—you'll burn the stable!"

"It's all right, old man," his companion said, grinning, "it ain't lit."

At this point the pipe smoker blew smoke from his mouth and made an angry remark in French which Maggie did not understand, but which Grandpa evidently did.

"*La pipe*," Grandpa repeated, sharply this time, "put it out now—*tout de suite!*"

"*Pourquoi?*" asked the smoker, grinning and removing his pipe.

"*C'est la loi!*" Grandpa pointed to a large, black-lettered sign on a red-painted board nailed to a post in plain sight. *DÉFENSE DE FUMER* it said in French in bold capital letters, and below that in smaller letters in English, "No Smoking."

The smoker dumped the still-smoldering ashes from his pipe into the chaff on the barn's dry board floor, then he slowly ground them out with the sole of his boot. "Satisfied?" he snarled in heavily accented English.

Grandpa walked off without answering.

🍂 🍂 🍂

That evening as usual, Grandpa was reading his Bible in his rocking chair by the kitchen stove, while Maggie was trying in vain to amuse herself with a chess game.

"Grandpa," she said at last, "you were talking French to that guy with the pipe. I didn't know you knew French."

"I don't, really." Grandpa put his Bible down and peered over his reading glasses. "But I've learned a few useful phrases out of necessity."

"Does *tout de suite* mean 'put your pipe out'?" Maggie wanted to know.

"*Tout de suite* means 'immediately,'" Grandpa answered. "And I'm afraid I was angry when I said it. *C'est la loi* means 'that's the law!'"

"Grandpa, why do we get angry so easily? I get mad at Jacky, but it doesn't make sense, does it? I was mad at him when I came here to live, and I was mad at him when he left this morning. Jacky's fun to be with, but when things go wrong, I blame him."

"I know," Grandpa said thoughtfully. "I could've prevented my angry confrontation with that hot-tempered young man if I'd 'a' used my head."

"But Grandpa, those guys were *rude*!

"True. But all I'd have had to do was to tell their foreman, who speaks English, that one of his men was smoking in the barn. He'd have stopped it at once."

"What's wrong with telling them yourself, like you did?"

"First, I acted in haste. Then again, young French

woodchoppers don't like takin' orders from an old *Anglais* like me."

"Why not?"

"Human nature. It would 'a' been the same if I'd been French, and they English. We're all sinners. I've been readin' that here in Paul's letter to the Romans. We resent being told what to do because it reminds us that we often do wrong, and that offends God, who made us."

"That's for sure," Maggie brightened.

"By acting hastily and telling him to put his pipe out *tout de suite*, I was acting in selfish pride, 'cause I wanted him to obey, and it wasn't my place."

"Like the waves of the sea obeyed Jesus," Maggie said, remembering a Bible story she'd heard long ago.

"Say, you *are* a very perceptive young lady. And that's right. Jesus is God, and only God had a right to demand immediate obedience to all His orders. The rest of us have this right only as God gives it. And those men must obey their boss, not me." He was quiet for a moment. "I must apologize to Jake for criticizing him next chance I get. I'm afraid I wasn't settin' you a very good example," he added quietly.

"I guess that explains why Jacky and I fight. We're tryin' to tell each other what to do."

"It sure does explain things," agreed Grandpa. "But there's a solution. We can choose to obey God in our lives each day. And that must begin by believing that when God sent His Son, Jesus Christ, to die on the cross for us, Christ's death is all we need to pay for our sins of pride and impatience. Then God will help us win over anger, temper, and disobedience in our lives."

Maggie left her chair and sat on the floor by Grandpa, resting her head on his knees. "Grandpa, I don't understand myself at all. I wanted to go home with Mama this morning, but I couldn't. I do want to like Jacky, but I can't when I'm mad at him."

"Jesus will solve that if you let Him," Grandpa quietly answered. He patted Maggie's head as she began to cry softly.

❧ ❧ ❧

"Grandpa, I've made some decisions," Maggie said next morning at breakfast.

"What are they?"

"I've given my anger to Jesus, and He's forgiven it all."

"And?"

"And I've decided I want to stay the rest of the winter with you, here at The Elms. I love this place, an' I love you," she said. "When I do go home, I'll enjoy it that much more."

Chapter 13

Eagle Lake Camp Detectives

Two days after Maggie's family left for Laketon and the loggers took their horses back to the camp, Maggie was surprised late in the afternoon to hear sleigh bells in the yard beside the verandah. She ran to the sitting room and looked through the curtains. There stood a tiny, brown-and-white horse hitched to a little sleigh barely wide enough for two small people. The driver, a slender person swaddled in a bearskin coat and a rabbit-fur cap and mittens, was bent over at the moment, tying the horse to the rail of the front steps.

Maggie tugged her sweater tightly about her and stepped onto the verandah. The rig's driver was trotting up the steps as quickly as if she lived there.

"Maggie!" Marie exclaimed, and she rushed to give her a hug.

"Marie . . . why, why I didn't expect to see you till the tug ran again after the lake thaws in the spring! And wherever did you get that *darling* horse? He's so tiny!" She motioned toward the long-maned pony hitched to the red sleigh. "What's his name?"

"Charlemagne. He belongs to the camp. *Maman* uses him sometimes to run errands."

"But you came alone!"

111

"Of course!" Marie's dark eyes flashed merrily. Framed in the white hood of rabbit fur, Maggie thought she'd never seen her friend look so beautiful. "Marie is the big girl now. Besides," she said impishly, "the woodchoppers, they look out for me."

"There are no loggers around here. I don't understand," Maggie said.

"They are cutting the east slope of the ridge between Lake Allagash and Lake Chamberlain," Marie explained. "Once I cross that ridge to the west slope, you can see me from The Elms," she said, pointing to a faint trail winding uphill through the trees in the distance on the far side of the lake. "So *Maman* said that since I am never out of sight of someone to watch, I can come. You not think Marie going to wait all winter to learn the books, *non*?"

"*Oui*," Maggie agreed. "Let's get your little horse in the barn and get you inside. You must be cold."

"Not horse—pony, a Shetland pony."

"I've never seen one before," Maggie admitted. "But I've heard of 'em. But they really *are* horses, aren't they?"

"Horse—*non*; pony," Marie insisted.

Maggie opened her mouth to point out that Charlemagne certainly looked to her like a miniature horse; he surely wasn't an ox. But something deep within her told her to say no more, lest she hurt her friendship with Marie. Maggie had learned bitter lessons about friendship during her week with Jacky. Besides, something or Someone had changed her life.

"Are ponies really horses, *Grand-père*?" Maggie was surprised at Marie's question to Grandpa Fuller at supper. She was glad, too, that she had not attempted to force her opinion upon Marie.

"Many folks don't think so," Grandpa mildly observed. "They are very unusual in Maine, except as show animals at fairs and circuses. But I think you'll find the groom at the horse stables at Eagle Lake Camp would call your Shetland a *petit cheval*."

"A small horse," said Maggie, who was beginning to learn a few words of French. She waited politely for Grandpa to continue.

"The Shetland pony is indeed a small horse bred in the rugged Shetland Islands off the coast of Scotland," Grandpa explained. "Farms there are tiny, unlike the large farms we have in Maine or in Quebec where you are from, Marie. So over hundreds of years these small animals were developed by selective breeding to plow the islands' tiny fields. But in America, these animals are a novelty. By the way, what's his name?"

Grandpa laughed aloud when Marie answered, "Charlemagne."

"What's so funny?"

"Well . . . I . . . it's just that it seems odd to give a *small* horse a name that means 'Charles the Great,' that's all. Of course Charlemagne was a great French king, and your Charlemagne certainly is a noble animal."

"Oh!" Marie was surprised. "I didn't know he was named after a king. Now I like him even better."

❦ ❦ ❦

Marie's two days' stay at The Elms was over all too soon, Maggie thought. The morning she was to leave, as they were finishing breakfast, Marie fished a small white envelope from a pocket in the wool knickers she had worn for the trip. It was sealed with wax and smelled faintly of perfume. She passed the envelope to Maggie.

"What *ever* could this mean?" Maggie asked in surprise, noticing "*Mlle*. Maggie Ridlon" penned neatly in black script on the outside. Carefully she lifted the wax seal with a table knife. Within she found a small formal card with a note in black ink:

> Dear *Mlle*. Ridlon,
>
> Please honor us with your pleasant company for a week at Eagle Lake Camp. Marie has asked to bring you home with her in the sleigh.
>
> We will get you a ride home after your stay, if Marie cannot bring you back.
>
> Affectionately,
>
> *Mme*. Evangeline LaRochelle

"Does *Madame* LaRochelle think my first name is Millie?" Maggie asked in concern, then quickly she added, "Oh, Marie, of course I'll go back with you, if it's all right with Grandpa!"

"It's all right with your old grandpa," Grandpa chuckled. Then seeing Marie's quizzical look about Maggie's first remark, he added, "That's your French lesson for today, Maggie. M-l-l-e is the abbreviation for *mademoiselle*, which is the same as *Miss* in English. M-m-e stands for *madame*."

The three laughed together.

❧ ❧ ❧

Marie wrapped Charlemagne in a heavy brown wool blanket before she hitched him to the sleigh.

"The breeze across the lake will make him shiver," she explained, as she and Maggie climbed aboard.

The girls found themselves wedged together so tightly they could not tuck the buffalo robe by themselves, so Grandpa tucked them in. He then rolled the barn's tall front door open. "Hup!" Marie cried, slapping the reins. Charlemagne strained, slowly dragging the sleigh across the dry board floor, then he broke into a trot as the steel runners hit the slippery snow.

Pony, sleigh, and passengers shot around the house, and as the path pitched downhill toward the lake, Marie pulled the reins tighter to slow Charlemagne to a walk. As her pony reached the level lake, Marie let the reins hang loose, letting the beast run at his own gait. Maggie felt the sharp, below-zero breeze biting her cheeks as they sped along.

Presently Marie passed the reins to Maggie. "Want to drive?"

"Could I?"

"Sure. Just keep him pointed toward that logging road on the far side of the lake."

"What do I say? Does Charlemagne understand English?"

"Just steer him with the reins. If you want to stop, holler, 'Whoa!'"

Charlemagne stopped.

Maggie slapped the reins and shouted, "Gid-dap!" at the top of her lungs. Charlemagne refused to budge.

"Hup, boy, hup!" Marie shouted as soon as she got over a fit of laughter. "There's just two words that animal understands, and you musn't use either unless you want him to respond," Marie explained.

Three-quarters of an hour's brisk trot brought the girls across the lake. "Whoa," cried Maggie. Obediently, Charlemagne stopped.

The pony waited patiently as Marie removed his blanket. It was warmer, now, for the sun had begun to climb higher. "Besides," Marie explained, "since we're goin' uphill for quite a ways, he'll sweat if I leave the blanket on."

The logging trail led through a thicket of Christmas tree-sized balsam firs. Here and there a tall, ragged white pine towered above the underbrush, and smaller white pines were seen struggling to grow straight among the firs.

"The loggers left those old pines to reseed this hillside," Marie explained. "The firs came up first, but they are needed to crowd the pines and force them to grow straight an' tall."

"That's sorta like people, Grandpa says," Maggie replied thoughtfully. "We need others around to straighten us out. I came to The Elms from Laketon to get away from people I didn't like. Grandpa says maybe God's sent me some other people to help *me* grow straight."

"Your *grand-père* sounds a lot like my *maman*," Marie laughed. "She says she'd rather have you to play with me even if we fight, than have me makin' a pest o' myself around the kitchen."

"Whoa!" Pony and sleigh now topped the ridge, and Marie pulled their rig to a halt. Perhaps a hundred yards downhill two loggers had felled a tall white pine. Maggie spied a crosscut saw, perhaps eight feet long, which lay reflecting the morning sun across the pine's stump, broad as a dining room table. Two men, their shirts removed to reveal the tops of their red union suits, chopped the limbs from the tree with axes, the pompons on their stocking caps switching in time with their swinging.

Further down the hillside Maggie spied a third man wearing a wool mackinaw. He was using a pair of gray Percheron workhorses to haul off logs other choppers had felled.

"We've gotta wait here till the guys finish limbing this tree an' cut it in half with their saw. Then the horse driver'll haul it out of our way," Marie said. "Charlemagne needs a rest, anyway."

Far below the girls lay the north end of Chamberlain Lake, and between two low hills, Maggie could see the broad white expanse of snow that was Eagle Lake. Beyond the northernmost hill rose a column of steam and smoke that she pointed to as they waited. "Is that Eagle Lake Camp?"

"Sure is. I can see that *Maman's* kitchen is goin' full blast."

🍂 🍂 🍂

We've got a theft problem around here, girls," Evangeline LaRochelle remarked, opening the root cellar door. Maggie, who had never seen so much food in her life, stared in disbelief. Hams by the dozens hung on leather thongs in this long building that was partly underground, in the hillside behind the camp's kitchen. Perhaps a hundred whole sides of bacon hung from the rafters, the thongs that the butcher had slipped through the corner of each one for smoking now looped over a nail. There were a huge bin of potatoes, shelves crowded with rutabagas, which the Canadians called turnips, along with hundreds of huge Danish baldhead cabbages.

Madame LaRochelle pointed to a bare nail in a rafter. "Last night a side of bacon hung there," she said. "This morning it was gone. Two days ago we lost a ham. But so far, no canned goods on the kitchen shelves have been stolen."

Maggie sniffed the air. The odor of hams and bacon made her hungry. She was glad that lunch would soon be ready.

"The ones closest to the shelves have been taken," Marie noticed at once. "So it must have been a short person, and he needed something to climb."

"I can't reach any of them," said Marie's *maman*. "So I step up on a plank shelf or use the stool."

Maggie rushed ahead suddenly and leaped at a ham. She touched it easily with her fingertips. "Marie's right," she said decidedly. "A taller man would simply lift a piece of meat off a nail and walk away."

"Let's see about that," added *Maman*. "Guy," she called. Guy, the cook's helper, appeared at once. He was a slender man of medium build, though several inches taller than Marie's *maman*. "Slice up a side of bacon for tomorrow's breakfast, *s'il vous plaît*. That one," she said, pointing to a bacon slab that hung higher than the rest.

"*Oui, Madam*." Guy easily picked the bacon off its nail, stretching himself only slightly.

"*Merci beaucoup*," *Madame* LaRochelle murmured, as Guy carried the bacon toward the kitchen. To the girls she said, "That narrows the list of suspects considerably. But we do have several short men on the logging crew."

"Marie, did you know that a famous poet, Edgar Allen Poe, once wrote a detective story, *The Murders in the Rue Morgue*? It's in Grandpa's library," Maggie said during dinner. Suddenly it occurred to her that the "Case of the Bacon Thief" might, like Poe's mystery story, also be unusual.

"What's a de-teck-tiff?"

"Detective," Maggie corrected. "Anyway, I've got an idea."

"Which is?" Marie wasn't sure she trusted Maggie's eagerness.

"The moon should be out tonight. We could sleep up there, by that window." Maggie pointed to a storage loft above the kitchen. "We'll take turns sittin' up an' watchin'."

"I dunno," said Marie. "S'pose the thief saw us an' got mean?"

"Oh, Marie. You said yourself that none of the men in this camp would hurt you, even though they tease you."

"You're right, I guess, Maggie. Now I've got an idea. Why don't we get some sleep before supper? That way we can stay awake tonight, *non?*"

That evening at dusk Maggie and Marie found *Madame* LaRochelle securing the root cellar by dropping a small beam across brackets on either side of the cellar's double doors. She then hammered a nail into either side of the door, clinching them against the beam. "There," she declared, "that won't stop the thief, but he'll have t' make racket enough to wake you *filles* if he wants t' get in."

A light snow fell that evening, stopping about midnight. The full moon peeped through the clouds from time to time, and the girls could see that the root cellar was still secure. When the snow ceased, the clouds parted, and the moon illuminated things so that not even a mouse could scurry past without being seen.

But, bright as the night was for catching crooks, both girls fell asleep. They woke only when they heard *Maman* and Guy rattling the stove lids in the kitchen below.

But there were no tracks in the snow, and snow lay lightly on the beam across the door, so they could see it hadn't been disturbed.

"We'll wait again tonight," Maggie said confidently, as she and Marie chopped boiled potatoes for breakfast hash.

"*Madame!*" cried Guy suddenly, "the bacon—another one is gone!"

The girls rushed out after *Maman*. Sure enough, another nail that had held a side of bacon was empty.

"They didn't go through," said Maggie in her most professional tone, "so they must have gone around."

"There is no around," protested Guy. "The cellar goes into the hillside."

Marie rushed outside at Maggie's suggestion, however. "*Maman!*" she called. "Maggie an' Guy, come here!" Marie had found a tunnel dug under the cellar's log wall, just where the building went into the hill. It was large enough for a very small person—one who would need to climb on the shelves to reach the bacon—to crawl through. Whoever had stolen the bacon had covered his tracks in the snow by dragging something after him.

"Why didn't we spot the tunnel inside?" Maggie wondered, as she and Marie followed the trail through the woods.

"'Cause it comes out under a bottom shelf, silly," retorted Marie.

Maggie bent to pick up a short leather thong as she hurried after Marie, dropping it into her pocket.

The trail ended at a horse road. All trace of further dragging had been destroyed by a pung and horses that had passed before dawn.

After breakfast, Maggie remembered the rawhide thong, which she showed to Marie. It smelled like bacon.

"It's a strap for hanging bacon, all right, Maggie. But what about it?"

"Does your *maman* have a magnifying glass?"

"*Oui*. She keeps one in her medicine kit for finding splinters in the men's hands."

"What do you see?" Marie asked, as a few minutes later Maggie examined the thong by a kitchen window.

"I'm not sure. Please get me a knife." Maggie cut the thong in half, then she looked intently at the cut ends.

"What *do* you see?" Marie insisted.

"Look here—all very scientific."

Marie looked through the glass. "Why, Maggie, you did it!"

"Yep. That thong was gnawed off by a rodent. The knife cuts don't look the same—they're more even. Like in Poe's detective story in which the murderer was a gorilla, the evil work in the root cellar was done by an animal!"

Chapter 14

Evangeline's Story

The next day Maggie and Evangeline LaRochelle were examining the thief Guy had caught in a wooden box trap, when it paid another midnight visit to the hillside pantry for a feast of ham or bacon. It was the biggest, fattest ring-tailed raccoon Maggie had ever laid eyes on, now imprisoned in a wire cage which Guy had hastily improvised when Maggie had shown him the evidence that their burglar was a rodent. The animal raced back and forth, frantically trying to escape, ignoring the strips of bacon rind and cabbage leaves Guy had given it for food.

"A couple of the loggers cut down a hollow coon tree near here a couple of weeks ago," Guy explained, chuckling. "They caught the female, but the male, he got away. They disturbed his long sleep, an' he's been robbing the root cellar ever since."

"That coon reminds me of myself," Evangeline said sadly as soon as Guy had gone into the kitchen.

"How so?" Maggie asked in concern.

"I . . . I've never been free, except in my heart. But you could not understand, *non*?"

Maggie was caught quite by surprise by *Madame* LaRochelle's frank comment.

"You mean you're not free here?"

"Ah, Maggie, if you only knew. I love my work, an' the men, they are good to me. They have such big appetites, and they say kind things about my cooking. But the lumber camp, she is no place to raise a girl, *non*?"

"But then why are you here?"

"That's a story. It goes back to when I was your age. My *père*—my papa—he died an' left my *maman* a widow. Kind missionaries, they come to our house in Quebec City, an' they give *Maman* a Bible. But *Maman* could not read, so I read. Night after night I read the Bible in French. Never before have I seen a French Bible—only written in *anglais*."

"In the Bible I learned of Jesus, how He died on the cross to set me free from jealousy an' hate an' anger an' greed—all these sins an' many more. So I ask Jesus to set me free, an' He does, an' I am happy."

"I asked Jesus to be my Savior, too," Maggie said quietly. "Just a few weeks ago."

"Oh, Maggie," cried Evangeline, hugging her tightly, "then perhaps you *do* understand."

"I understand what you mean about jealousy, anger, and also pride," said Maggie. "I've been jealous of my stepbrother, Jacky. And for a time my pride wouldn't let me be happy when I saw that Marie was catching up with me in reading. But Jesus has helped me overcome that, though I do sometimes slide back into my old ways. But what happened to you after your papa died?"

"*Maman* and I met this logger, Pierre LaRochelle—we called him Pete."

Maggie held her breath at this. She already knew that Pierre LaRochelle was Marie's father.

"'Pete,' *Maman* used to say, 'you are too old to cut logs.' But Pete had found a job as a horse driver for the loggers here in this very camp, at *Lac* Eagle. A horse driver must work hard and put in long hours, but the work is not back-breaking, like cutting with a saw and an axe."

"So how did you become Pete's wife?" Maggie asked in wonder.

"Marie has already told you he was her father, *non?*" Evangeline answered. "Well, no matter. I wanted to go to school, but my *maman*, being a widow, had no money for academy tuition. Oh, I had lots of books, in French and *anglais* and Latin, even. I still buy books on nature and teach Marie all I can. *Maman* would say I devour books. Our parish priest, he said I should go to university in Montreal, but first I should go to convent and become a nun. Perhaps they would send me to the university, if they saw I had potential. I could become a teaching sister, maybe."

"Why didn't you?" Maggie wasn't sure if becoming a nun was what Evangeline should have done. But she felt she had to ask.

"Pete, he say that I should marry him, if *Maman* would consent. Lots of girls my age were married in those days," she said sadly. "And Pete owned a team of Clydesdale horses. They are better horses than any the logging company owns, an' he could make good money leasing them to the company and driving them himself. He could soon earn more money and buy more horses, or a farm, maybe."

"So you married Pete? How old were you?"

"How *old*? You mean how *young!*" Evangeline laughed. "I was fourteen and Pete was forty-eight. No girl that young should even look at a boy."

"But Pete wasn't a *boy.* He was a man—almost an *old* man," Maggie protested.

"Maggie," Evangeline said quietly, slowly, gently, "I soon learned to love Pete LaRochelle. He loved me and gave me Marie. Our life was tough, but we had our happinesses. Then one day when Marie was still small they brought his body back to the camp on his pung drawn by his own horses, those beautiful horses! He drove under a tree the loggers were felling. It killed him instantly." Evangeline sat down on a log by the raccoon's cage, and covering her face with her apron, she began to sob.

Maggie sat next to this woman of the woods, young, beautiful, and so like Maggie's own mother. Maggie recalled how happy Mother was with John Hanscombe—how she smiled and sang in the kitchen again. *Perhaps a man will marry Evangeline and take her away from her life of drudgery in the camp*, she thought.

"*Madame* LaRochelle—Evangeline," Maggie said, "you have been a great help to me."

"Have I? How?" she asked in surprise.

"You have helped me see that my troubles are small, compared to others'. And you have helped me to appreciate my own mother and her new husband."

"I do wish every day to be of help to someone. God has put that in my heart."

"Your name, you know—it is really interesting."

"Oh?" Evangeline was surprised.

"My grandpa told me that *Evangeline* means angel or evangelist, or messenger from God. You have brought me a message from God today."

"I'm so glad you found something good in my name, and in what I said, too. But I must get to work.

The men will be wanting their dinner," Evangeline said, rising to her feet.

"What happened to Pete's Clydesdales?" Maggie asked, as she strolled with Evangeline toward the kitchen.

"I sold them at once and put the money in the bank. Every year I take some out to pay my *maman's* taxes on her house in Quebec City. Someday that house will be mine and Marie's, but *Maman* will lose it if I don't pay the taxes."

"Does Marie want to go to school?"

"That's the hardest part. I could send Marie to school with the money from the sale of the horses," she sighed, "but we must keep it for the taxes."

Chapter 15

The Timber Cruiser

Spring arrives in late April in the Maine woods, or not even until early May, a full month after the rest of New England thaws out. It was mid-April, in fact, when Grandpa Fuller finally pulled his fishing shanty off the ice of Allagash Lake and warned Maggie, "The ice is gettin' white an' punky. So stay off it. We'll do more pickerel fishin' next winter."

Then comes "mud season"—nearly a month of thawing days, rain, and sometimes sleet. Canoes cannot cross the lakes because of the ice cakes. Horses cannot travel the forest roads because of the muck, so the men who cut the logs must leave them where they lay until the woods dry out. Folks traveling on foot had wet feet and soggy pants, for there were no rubber boots in those days. Only for the direst emergencies did most folks venture far from home.

So, after weeks of isolation, without having seen Marie since March, Maggie peered down the lake one merry May morning and saw that it was again free of ice and smooth as glass. "When's the tugboat goin' to run again, Grandpa?" she asked. "I haven't seen Marie in a coon's age."

"Likely be June, July maybe. Comp'ny won't run

the tug till they get logs enough t' make it pay. Costs money t' put that boat in the water."

"Grandpa," Maggie asked, "could I take the small canoe over to Eagle Lake Camp? It's only a couple of hours, an' I'll stay close to the shore as I paddle. I know the way."

"Well ... well, I promised your ma that I'd keep you in one piece." He paused. Maggie waited, and even the striking of the tall clock did not drown out the beating of her heart.

"Well, since you put it that way—an' you're a teen-ager now, which is almost grown up, you can go. How 'bout for three days? I'd let you stay a week, like in January, but in another week the no-see-ums an' skee-ters'll be so thick you could make a soup without a kettle."

Grandpa did not say so, but he really did not wish to wait a week to know if Maggie were alive or drowned in the lake. His observation about the spring insect infestation, Maggie knew, was correct. The swamps and bogs around Laketon were impossible to travel in after three or four days of warm weather.

❦ ❦ ❦

"Who is that boy two tables over?" Maggie asked Marie her first evening at Eagle Lake Camp.

"Well," giggled Marie, "I can see 'bout twenty boys. There's Henri, an' Jean, an' Louis, an' Gilbert. Perhaps you were looking at Fredric, or Victor— Vallery, maybe?"

"Oh, cut it out. Those are all *men*. Who's the *boy*, the one with the sandy hair and freckles—the one who's *not* French?"

"Oh, him? You must mean the new timber cruiser. They call him Terry."

"Terry. I like the sound of that," Maggie admitted. "But what's a timber cruiser?"

"His job is to travel the length of the Allagash Wilderness, from Moosehead Lake to Fort Kent, and find stands of timber that are ready to cut for sawlogs. Then the sawmill's buyer deals with the landowners to buy standing trees. It's really an important job, 'cause the company decides how much to pay based on the timber cruiser's estimate of the quality of the timber."

"But he's so young!"

"He's twenty, and so—how do you say it in *anglais*?—mature!"

Maggie changed the subject and asked no more questions.

After supper as Maggie helped Marie and Guy clear the tables, they were entertained by music from a corner of the dining room. Several young woodchoppers sat in a half-circle singing. Some were playing mouth organs, one had an accordion, and another bent over his violin, which sang a tune sweeter than any bird. But all were seated facing a harmonica player in a chair in the corner.

Maggie caught sight of the player as one of the choppers got up to leave. It was the same sandy-haired Terry she'd noticed earlier. He tipped his chair against the wall, one foot on a rung, as he played an oversized harmonica with a double row of reeds, leading this spur-of-the-moment orchestra who followed his tunes faithfully.

The evening of Maggie's second day at Eagle Lake Camp she lay awake on her pallet in the loft of *Madame* LaRochelle's tiny cabin. The small gable window was swung wide open, and through the copper screening came the music of spring peepers from a marshy alcove of the lake, just under the hill from the dining hall/kitchen complex.

Silently Maggie slipped to the window and peered out. She could not see the lake because the cabin was behind the dining hall. Maggie then realized that the night music of the spring frogs was being echoed off the wall of the building next door. Suddenly she was seized with an urge to hear the songs of these nocturnal musicians close up.

Marie had been asleep for some hours, and Marie's *maman*, who had worked late in the kitchen, was now snoring in her bed at the foot of the ladder to the loft. Maggie grabbed her folded sweater, which she had been using to bolster her thin, pine needle-filled pillow, and tucked it under her arm. She clapped her soldier's cap on her head, adjusting it in the dark. Slowly she slid down the loft ladder, missing most of the rungs as she shinnied along.

Maggie paused by Evangeline's bedside long enough to fish a single match from the base of the kerosene lamp. She padded on bare feet to the reading table at the foot of the bed, where Evangeline kept her alarm clock out of reach so she'd have to get up when it went off at 5:00 A.M.

Did she dare? Maggie turned toward Evangeline's bed to see that she had not stirred. Shielding the match with her body, Maggie struck it on the table and held it to the clock. "Eleven-fifty."

As soon as Maggie was outdoors, she pulled her sweater over her flannel nightgown against the chill air of the spring evening. Grandma Ridlon had knitted this sweater, now a bit too small for Maggie. Though

Maggie had sometimes found Grandma Ridlon crotchety and complaining, she was thankful at times like these that she had a grandma who cared for her. But tonight Maggie was off on a venture of her own.

The loudest chirping seemed to be coming from near the spring above the marsh, where a windmill and an elevated water tank kept the camp supplied with mountain spring water. Her feet soon found the path leading up to the spring. She looked back but once—to glance toward the bunkhouses and make certain that the lamps were out and all was dark, for the men had long since gone to bed.

Maggie sat for a long time on the concrete platform under the windmill, her shoulder resting against a steel brace as she listened. Above the gurgle of the spring's outlet flowing over the spillway into the marsh, a million peeps came from every part of the marsh and along the lakefront beyond, filling the night air of early May with music. How glad Maggie was to be out on a night like this! Grandpa had rightly advised her that this time between winter and the warm evenings of later spring would be the only time free of flies and mosquitoes to enjoy the night sounds uninterrupted. There would be no more nights like this until the frosts of September put the biting insects to sleep for the winter.

Distinctly now her ears picked up a "chi-r-r-r-r-r-up, chi-r-r-r-r-r-up, chi-r-r-r-r-r-up" from almost beneath her feet, in a stagnant pool at the water's edge. She bent to investigate, and the chirping stopped. Maggie settled back against the tower brace, and the musical chirping began again, this time answered by another insistent chirping at the edge of the marsh, downhill from the tank and windmill tower.

Now deciding to investigate this second chirper, Maggie made her way along stones and gravel so cold they nearly numbed her bare feet. She approached a clump of alder bushes, still barren of leaves, where she stood still to listen. The "chi-r-r-r-r-up" of the frog by the water tower was now answered by a frog in the marsh, singing just an octave lower. Then a third tone, a reedy melody, caught her ear, mimicking both frogs. Long and high it sang, then long and low, perfectly pitched to each of the frogs' singing, though smoother, without the trill. Was it an insect? A bird, perhaps?

Maggie straightened up, intending to push her way along the water's edge behind the alders. But the clouds parted at that moment, and she saw her shadow cast in the moonlight against the hillside. At the same time a sharp breeze caught the skirts of her nightgown, and a chill ran through her body. Suddenly Maggie felt helpless and alone. Quickly she hurried back to the cabin and to her mat and blanket in the loft with Marie.

Next morning, as soon as breakfast was over, Marie helped Maggie pack a lunch and carry her things to her canoe at the waterfront on Eagle Lake.

"I'm comin' to The Elms in a couple of weeks whether the tug is running or not, if *Maman* will let me," promised Marie.

"Please do. An' thank your mother for me," Maggie said, pushing off.

"*Au revoir*," Marie cried, answering Maggie's, "Good-bye!"

❦ ❦ ❦

The grass was still wet with morning dew at the

portage between Eagle Lake and Chamberlain Lake, so Maggie slid her canoe along, happy for the help God had given to speed her on her journey.

Maggie had her own private thrill every time she and Grandpa crossed Chamberlain Lake, for this lake she would now soon cross was named for General Joshua Chamberlain. General Chamberlain had been Lieutenant Colonel Chamberlain until after the Battle of Gettysburg, and he was the commander of the Maine 20th Volunteers at Little Round Top, near Gettysburg, where Maggie's father, Sergeant Jim Ridlon of Company B, had died the year she was born.

As Maggie rounded the last bend in the trail, she saw a canoe by Chamberlain Lake. It was turned over, so evidently it had been there for some time.

Maggie was not afraid, though she was a bit nervous. The wilderness was not a dangerous place, Grandpa had assured her, but still Maggie did not enjoy meeting strangers so far from help. But the canoe, a trapper's model much larger than hers, was upturned, so she decided that the owner had gone off and was no doubt miles away.

"Well, well, so you're the sentry, the girl with the red hair!" The speaker had suddenly sat up beside his canoe as Maggie was bending over pushing hers into the water. His accent was anything but French. He rolled his R's like the family of Irish immigrants who had moved to Laketon shortly before Maggie had come to The Elms. Yet he didn't sound Irish, exactly.

"Sentry?" Maggie exclaimed as she suddenly straightened.

The speaker pointed to Maggie's blue military cap. "You surprised me last night by the spring, so I guess it's my turn to surprise you. I thought maybe Eagle

Lake Camp had hired a night watchman. But then army camp sentries and watchmen don't ordinarily wear nightgowns," he chuckled.

Maggie's freckles turned red.

"Pardon me. I'm Scottish myself," remarked the freckle-faced young man. "Ridlon's Scottish, is it not? It's Maggie, right?"

"How . . . how did you know?"

"Red hair is quite unusual in a lumber camp. So I asked *Madame* LaRochelle. How else?"

"You're the new timber cruiser!"

"You've been asking some questions yourself, evidently. Name's Terence MacAlester—friends call me Terry," he answered with a merry twinkle in his pale blue eyes. "And where are you from, Maggie?"

"I live with my grandfather, Bill Fuller, at The Elms, the company horse farm over on Allagash Lake, just a few miles west."

"Well, may I help you on your way? I paddled over here last night after listening to the peepers, so I could get an early start on my trip north. I must say I overslept. Thanks to you, I'm up and about."

Maggie sat down in her canoe, letting Terry push her smoothly into the waters of Chamberlain Lake. As she paddled off toward the second portage and Allagash Lake, she sang quietly under her breath:

> You take the high road,
> And I'll take the low road,
> And I'll be in Scotland afore ye;
> Me an' my true love will never meet again
> On the bonnie, bonnie banks of Loch
> Lomond.

Maggie paused in her singing as she paddled hard and pulled away. To her surprise, the strains of the lyrics she'd just sung floated clearly across the water in the reedy notes of a harmonica. Then the tune stopped, but the harmonica again sang, this time the trills of the peepers of the night.

Chapter 16

An American Thanksgiving

Why can't we make The Elms into a *real* farm, Grandpa?" Maggie asked one day shortly after returning from her visit with Marie at Eagle Lake Camp. "We have acres an' acres of land here that's nothing but horse pasture and hay fields. Why don't we plant some crops?"

"We've got over two hundred acres," chuckled Grandpa. "But I've got about all I can do tendin' these horses. When you see how busy we are this summer with my garden, an' in July with the hayin', you'll understand why an old man don't have time for row crops. Do you know how much hoeing there is in just one acre of corn?"

"I don't," admitted Maggie.

But two days later she found her answer. While scanning the titles in Grandpa's bookcase for an interesting book to read, her eye fell on *Agriculture in the Modern World*. It was a slender volume published by the U.S. Department of Agriculture. She took it down and found lots of steel-cut pictures and even a few photographs depicting various farming methods.

Maggie turned to the index in the back of the book. Sure enough, she found a section entitled, "Corn, Methods of Raising."

Perhaps this is what I need to convince Grandpa to plant corn, Maggie told herself as she carried the book, along with *Our Pilgrim Heritage,* up to her room.

Next morning Maggie was full of ideas at breakfast. "Grandpa, what do the loggers do on *American* Thanksgiving—the one in November?"

"Seems to me they do manage t' get an extra holiday," he chuckled. "Since a few of the crew are Americans, and this *is* the U.S.A., they give 'em *two* Thanksgiving Days. The Canadians don't seem t' mind!"

"But do they celebrate Thanksgiving, learning about the Pilgrims an' Squanto an' Captain Myles Standish an' Governor Bradford?" Maggie persisted.

"No, not really. The Americans that want to can go home, if they live close enough. The rest just get the day off," Grandpa admitted.

"No turkey or pumpkin pie?"

"No turkey, unless someone happens t' shoot a wild one. Pumpkin pie only if it happens t' be on the menu for dessert, I s'pose."

"Well, let's give Eagle Lake Camp a *real* Thanksgiving this fall. Here's my plan." Maggie held up the agriculture book, which she'd slipped under her chair before breakfast. She turned to the section on raising corn. "It says right here," she continued, "to plant your hills of corn eight feet apart, and around each hill plant a ring of pumpkin seeds. The pumpkin vines will spread out across the cornfield, so the weeds won't grow. An' since corn grows straight up, it towers above the vines, and they don't choke it out."

"Whoa, Maggie. I guess you've got me convinced about *raising* the crop," Grandpa responded. "I can sure use the extra corn for the cow. We do have a pair of good plow horses here, belongin' to the sawmill company. The fellows that come in July to cut the hay will use them on the mowing machine and rake. An' there's a horse-drawn plow in the tool shed, which used t' belong to the company president when he lived here. But after we harvest all those pumpkins, how're we goin' to get 'em made into pies?"

"Simple." Maggie looked at him with a grin.

"I don't get it."

"You said Eagle Lake Camp would serve for dessert whatever was on the menu. If I can convince *Madame* LaRochelle to serve pumpkin pie on American Thanksgiving Day, we can show 'em what a real Thanksgiving is like. An' I know Marie will help!"

Grandpa stroked his chin thoughtfully. "Y'know, the camp supply man once told me he'd buy any vegetables I could raise for his camps, because he could save money not havin' t' pay the freight from Central Maine. I'll just bet they'd be tickled pink t' haul those pumpkins t' Eagle Lake Camp on the tug. You'd have your American Thanksgiving, an' we'd make a few dollars of Christmas money in the bargain.

"Can we, Grandpa?"

"Most likely. Let me get some figures on paper. I'll need t' confirm this deal with the company buyer, an' then buy the seed. I've got to paddle over to headquarters in Millinocket next week, so it may work out. There's a farm store there that'll have plenty o' pumpkin seed. I need to buy seeds for the garden anyways," he concluded.

❧ ❧ ❧

Grandpa returned from Millinocket with the news that they could go ahead with the corn and pumpkin patch as planned. Maggie liked to work in the soil, so she pitched into this challenge with enthusiasm. One morning, as soon as breakfast was over, she found the wheelbarrow and a dung fork and was busily wheeling load after load of horse manure to the freshly plowed acre, dumping half a load where she'd marked off spots for hills of corn and pumpkins.

"You're doin' that the hard way, Maggie," remarked Grandpa, as he came from the barn where he had been feeding the horses, cow, and chickens.

"How else is there, Grandpa?"

"We've got a high, one-horse, two-wheeled cart in the barn. I can rig it up an' harness that gentle old mare to it, an' you can sit an' drive. So I'll load, an' you can just trot that mare out there an' pitch your load off where you want it."

Maggie and Grandpa took three more days to plant the corn and pumpkins, as well as rows of onions, beets, turnips, chard, beans, peas, radishes, and carrots in his garden. Grandpa put in a row of Kentucky Wonder pole beans, then squeezed in five tight rows of yellow-eyes, which, when dry would make delicious baked beans.

Maggie had to pull weeds almost daily, at first. But as the pumpkin vines grew and spread, the weeds were crowded out. Only here and there did a pigweed sprout up, which required her to wade into the scratchy vines to remove.

By early July the corn was knee high. In July, also, two young men arrived by canoe to cut the hay and store it in the barn. "I'll need to get a room ready and a bed made for those guys, won't I, Grandpa?" Maggie inquired, as soon as she realized why the men were there.

"No need. They're tired of bunkin' indoors," Grandpa explained. "Just give 'em three good meals an' plenty of switchel. They'd rather sleep in the hay-mow on the fresh clover an' grass."

Maggie awakened at four o'clock each morning for the next three weeks to the "click-click-click-click-click" of the mowing machine in the long fields sloping toward the woods behind the barn. The young men were up with the sun, and they wasted no time in harnessing the horses and getting to the field.

Breakfast she served at six, which was now usually oatmeal and eggs—potatoes would be in short supply until September. "They'll want coffee," Grandpa explained, so Maggie fixed a potful, a treat usually reserved for special guests.

Twice a day—more often if it was especially hot—Maggie made switchel. She would pour three-fourths of a cup of molasses, a third of a cup of vinegar, and a teaspoonful of ginger into a two-quart canning jar. Adding a quart of water, she would snap the lid on and shake vigorously until the molasses dissolved. Then she'd fill the jar the rest of the way with cold water from the outdoor pump and take it to the men in the field, leaving it beside the fence before scurrying back to the house.

By late afternoon the men would be ready to haul hay, and Grandpa and Maggie pitched in to help. Grandpa's job was to drive the horses at a walk, while the men pitched the hay over the sides of the rack. Maggie carried a handmade wooden pitchfork, which for the most part she used only to balance herself, as she packed down the loads of loose hay with her bare feet.

❦ ❦ ❦

In August, Grandpa resorted to chaining Bowser to a stake in the corn to ward off the coons who were eating the crops during the night. He figured that the hound, used to his freedom, would set up such a racket that no raccoon would venture within miles of the place. Bowser made a racket, all right. For two nights he cried so pitifully that, long after midnight, Maggie went out in her nightgown and set him free. He followed her to her room and slept on the foot of her bed until dawn.

On the third night, Maggie, seeing the destruction each morning in the corn—though the pumpkins were unharmed—determined to let him stay in the garden. But, having got his mistress's attention with his baying and yelping two nights in a row, poor Bowser decided to do so again. Maggie stayed in bed.

Grandpa Fuller, however, with his window open that August evening, rose from bed and lit a lamp. He loaded his gun and went out. Bowser had made a circle around his stake the length of his chain, Grandpa discovered, destroying the pumpkins and most of the corn as he ran around and around.

Just outside Bowser's trampled area sat a fat raccoon, saucily and greedily devouring an ear of half-ripe corn.

Next day Grandpa skinned the coon for its pelt and gave Maggie the tail to tie onto her army hat. "That hound's doin' more harm to the garden than the coons," Grandpa observed that evening as he cleaned his gun and trimmed the wick on his lamp. "He destroys the pumpkin vines wherever he drags his chain. The coons eat the ears, but they don't hurt the pumpkins, an' they do leave the cornstalks so's we can feed them to Molly, at least. 'Sides, buckshot won't hurt the garden any, either."

❦ ❦ ❦

Maggie's acre produced a bumper crop of pumpkins, which she and Grandpa loaded into the horse cart in early October and hauled to the woodshed to protect from freezing. On Monday before Thanksgiving, the tugboat anchored near The Elms' beach to load the pumpkins. Maggie climbed aboard, and they were off. "I'll be over in the canoe Thursday mornin'," Grandpa shouted above the "chuff-chug, chuff-chug" of the tug's steam engine.

Marie and Guy met Maggie and the tug at Eagle Lake Camp's dock with Charlemagne hitched to a cart. By suppertime the pumpkins were piled into the kitchen, along with a pail of Molly's Jersey cream for whipping.

There were no pies like those baked by Evangeline LaRochelle for the American Thanksgiving at Eagle Lake Camp in 1876. Maggie, Marie, Guy, and two other helpers split, cleaned, and boiled pumpkins until they smelled pumpkins in their dreams. Eggs by the dozens, milk by the pailful, and many pounds of sugar and spices went into a wooden vat that Evangeline stirred with a canoe paddle. Maggie rolled pastry until her arms were sore. "Thanksgiving's the day the guys get to have all the pie they want," she exclaimed.

And they *did* have turkey, real wild turkey, though not enough for everyone, but no matter. Several of the men carried their rifles and shotguns to the logging sites during hunting season and brought back such game as they could find. There were always several fat deer hanging in the root cellar, as fine as those the Indians furnished the Pilgrims for the first Thanksgiving, and many of the men preferred venison to turkey.

Salt codfish, too, in a white sauce made with flour, milk, and butter, made the men's mouths water, as they ladled it over boiled potatoes. Codfish had been a staple of diets in New England and eastern Canada for more than three hundred years, and all knew that the Pilgrims must certainly have enjoyed it.

Supper over, *Madame* LaRochelle stood on a chair and banged on a kettle with a wooden spoon. "*Mademoiselle* Maggie Ridlon," she cried as soon as she had the men's attention, "has brought us the pumpkins for the pies. She is going to make a speech about the Pilgrims and American Thanksgiving."

"Do they understand English?" Maggie whispered, fighting last-minute stage fright.

"Most of them understand some *anglais*. Now get up there and speak up!" Evangeline encouraged.

"More than two and a half centuries ago the Pilgrims came to Cape Cod in New England to escape religious persecution in the Old World," Maggie said in a speech she had written and memorized by saying it aloud to Bowser. "Because of their Christian beliefs," she continued, "they were driven out of their land.

"In the New World they found a spot where no people were living. Two Indians who could speak English, Samoset and Squanto, helped them out and showed them how to plant Indian crops, such as corn and pumpkins. That's why we have pumpkin pie for Thanksgiving!"

The men cheered and clapped. "*Encore, encore!*" several shouted.

Maggie bowed and continued: "All was not easy for these hardy Pilgrims. Half of them died the first winter. But in the spring when their hired ship, the *Mayflower*, sailed back to England, all decided to stay here.

"Because they loved God and their neighbors, when they were introduced to the Indian chief, Massasoit, they made a treaty that was unbroken for more than fifty years.

"Today we remember what these faithful people stood for by a day of thanksgiving. The Pilgrims' governor, William Bradford, first proclaimed Thanksgiving Day in 1621. Indians and white men sat down together in peace to thank God for His blessings. In 1863, the year that I was born, President Lincoln proclaimed a day of thanksgiving, which we have been celebrating every year ever since. As did those Pilgrims and Indians so long ago, let us, Americans and Canadians together, sit down in peace."

Marie's dark eyes shone with delight as she congratulated Maggie after her speech. "This has been a real Thanksgiving," she said. "Maggie and Marie will keep Thanksgiving together always, *non?*"

Chapter 17

Home for Christmas

As Grandpa and Maggie canoed back to The Elms on the Friday morning after Thanksgiving, Maggie noticed that the shallow coves along the lakeshore were already covered with ice and that a ring of ice formed on her paddle just above the water as she dipped it into the lake.

Soon, Maggie knew, there would be no more canoe trips, and that made her sad—blue, in fact. Already the tug had ceased to run. It would be after Christmas, when the lake was frozen solid, before Marie could travel with Charlemagne and his sleigh across the long expanses of ice and snow. Then, if heavy snows came in January, Maggie and Grandpa might be isolated at The Elms until March or even April.

When they arrived home at noon, Grandpa grabbed the milk pail and dashed toward the shed door where Molly the cow was waiting. "Get some chow on the table while I'm in the barn, will you, please?" he said. "I'll be back in 'bout an hour."

Tired as she was, Maggie tossed her knapsack into Grandpa's rocker and hurried to the range to build a cooking fire. She checked the woodbox, but she found only large pieces of oak and maple. In disgust, Maggie scurried into the woodshed. Finding an unsplit junk of dry cedar, she placed it on the chopping block and worked it over viciously with the hatchet.

But the cedar would not cooperate. The junk split, all right, but the pieces flew to the far corners of the woodshed. She gathered an armload and trudged angrily back to the kitchen. As soon as the fire was crackling—reluctantly, Maggie observed—she lit a lantern and headed for the cellar.

In a barrel sawed in half and filled with dry sand Maggie dug for carrots. Next, from the potato bin she selected six good-sized ones for boiling. They'd eat only two, but the other four would be sliced for frying later in the spider. Maggie then pulled a slab of bacon from its hook on the ceiling and dropped it into the basket with the vegetables.

The kindling was burning well when Maggie returned upstairs. She rammed two bolts of dry maple into the stove, then put on a pot of water for the potatoes. She scrubbed the potatoes, cut them in half, and dropped them into the water. Then she set to slicing carrots. These she added to the potato pot.

The bacon slab on the butcher block was being examined by Bowser, whom she had not fed since they had left the camp that morning. She cut him a piece of rind to chew on, then proceeded to slice off a dozen thick slices, being careful to get as much lean meat as possible. A thirteenth slice she cut, thicker than the rest, and tossed it to her hungry hound.

The spider now hot, Maggie slapped the slices of bacon into the pan, then set the table.

She turned to the dumbwaiter to bring some cold milk up from the cellar and sent the unsliced bacon back down. By now the bacon was done, so Maggie forked it onto a platter.

A terrible smell assailed Maggie's nose when she lifted the lid on the pot to inspect the boiling vegetables. She hadn't put in enough water, and they were burned.

Moments later, when Grandpa shuffled into the kitchen with a pail of warm milk, he found Maggie curled up in his rocker sobbing, her knapsack pushed onto the floor. "Don't make such a big deal over burnt potatoes, honey," he said gently. "There's half a loaf of bread in the cupboard, an' the stove's plenty hot. We can have toast an' bacon for lunch."

"It . . . it's not the burnt potatoes," Maggie said, her sobs softer now. "It's just . . . it's just that that *wasn't* Thanksgiving."

"Well, I don't know what you would call it. We had pumpkin pie an' you gave a speech, an' the men seemed to enjoy it."

"I know, Grandpa. And I liked doing it, but *Thanksgiving's* when you get together with your family. I know I don't have much family, and I do have *you*, Grandpa. But when I was small, you and Grandma Fuller used t' come, an' Grandma Ridlon, and sometimes Mama's cousins from Foxcroft. Then at Christmas, usually it was just Mother an' me, 'cause there was too much snow t' travel that far. But we'd go to the Christmas program at Laketon Community Church an' stay for the hymn sing afterward."

"When your mama was small, we used to go to church every Sunday," Grandpa said. After a long pause, he added, "As you know, your mama and her John and Jacky have started goin' t' church reg'lar again."

"I know. And I'd like to. Since . . . since I gave my heart to Jesus it seems like the place to be on Sunday."

"Well, we do take Sunday off around here. I spend part of each Sunday readin' God's Word an' prayin'." He ran his fingers through Maggie's tousled hair. "I think things are goin' t' be different from now on."

"I . . . I want to go home—home for Christmas!"

Grandpa was silent for a long time. Finally he said, "Your mama sent a letter, which the tug operator gave me while you were loadin' pumpkins. She's writin' you, too. It'll come by courier next week, prob'ly. But she asked me t' tell you myself, an' I been puttin' it off. Your folks can't come to The Elms for Christmas this year. John's work at the store won't let him, since business has been slack an' they can't afford extra help."

Maggie sat up. "I'm going home!"

"Now?" Grandpa was startled.

"No, no, Grandpa," Maggie laughed, her mood lifting. "Not now, but in time for Christmas."

"Well, I guess we can manage," the old man said hesitantly.

🎄 🎄 🎄

On Monday, just after noon, Maggie looked up from putting the dishes away to see a man in a trapper's deerskin coat and beaver-fur hat pull a canoe onto the beach.

Tossing his paddle into the canoe, he walked directly toward the verandah. As he disappeared from view, Maggie noticed that, instead of the green wool pants worn by most trappers and loggers, this man wore elegant moleskin breeches, and below these, a fine-looking pair of high cut boots of the sort worn by horseback-riding foremen on logging crews.

There came a brisk knock at the door. Maggie, tossing her apron across a chair, hurried to answer it.

"Is this The Elms, the fabled mansion of the Allagash?" jovially inquired the freckled stranger.

"Sir . . . Mr. MacAlester," Maggie stammered. "Come in."

"Terry," he corrected, his eyes twinkling. "Is Bill Fuller around?"

"He's in the barn—I'll get him."

"No need," Grandpa's voice crackled from the kitchen. "Give Terence a seat by the sittin' room stove. I'll be there soon's I wash up. And Maggie, fix us some coffee—all three of us, please. An' bring some o' them doughnuts you made Saturday."

"Your granddaughter makes good doughnuts," Terry remarked as soon as he'd bitten into one. "Sour cream?" he asked, turning to Maggie.

"Yes," Maggie said shyly.

"You're walkin' on thin ice, ain't ya, travelin' by canoe this late in the season?" Grandpa asked. "What brings you here, anyway?"

"If I'm not back to Eagle Lake Camp by dark, I'm in trouble," Terry admitted. "I just came into Allagash Lake from Allagash Stream—stayed last night at Cook Camp, up north. Lake's starting to skin over with ice already. By nightfall it'll be thick enough to tear holes in my canoe.

"I've spent the fall looking for locations for new logging camps north of here," he continued. "I've found half a dozen good spots, and lots of good saw timber. Thought you'd like to know." He drained his cup and rose to leave. "Gotta go before I'm frozen in."

"Say, what're you doin' this winter?" Grandpa inquired as they walked to the door.

Terry shrugged. "Scaling logs for the crews, probably. I'm wintering at Eagle Lake Camp."

"And over Christmas?"

"Get bored. Play checkers with whoever's left in the bunkhouse, read a few books, I suppose. Why?" He raised a bushy eyebrow.

"Maggie and I'd kinda like to have Christmas with our family in Laketon. Are you good with horses?"

"Love 'em!"

"Just one problem. I'll have a fellow here—an old trapper. He can tend a few, but I can't trust him with a whole barnful. But he'll want you to believe he's the boss."

"Old Jake? I met the chap this morning. He was running his trap line. We'll get along," he chuckled.

"Then you'll do it?"

"Sure. Pay me what you think it's worth—that's no Scottish bargain!" he laughed. Terry wrinkled his nose. "I like the smell of this place a lot better than those bunkhouses full of tobacco smoke," he said. With a wink at Maggie he added, "Can y' keep a secret? Your doughnuts are as good as Evangeline LaRochelle's—maybe better!"

❦ ❦ ❦

The day before Christmas, Maggie and Grandpa Fuller left before dawn by moonlight for the long hike over frozen trails to catch the train at the sawmill, the frozen moss creaking under their boots as they trudged along in the brisk December air. Maggie soon discovered that Grandpa was not as merciless in his marching as he was in his paddling. "Let's rest," he would frequently announce, finding a log to sit on as he massaged his aching knees. But by noon they had reached the sawmill and found seats in the caboose behind a long string of flatcars loaded with lumber.

"Why did Terry MacAlester stop at The Elms last month to tell you about his trip north?" Maggie asked as the train rolled south toward Laketon.

"Openin' loggin' camps up north means The Elms will be closed as a horse farm," explained Grandpa.

"This year?"

"Hard t' say," Grandpa said, brushing off Maggie's query. "Maybe—maybe next year. But we can be sure God had *His* reasons for Terence stoppin'. I couldn't have left Jake with that many horses while we took this trip," he mused. "I sure hope Katherine's John is waitin' for us at the depot with a horse an' sleigh," he added, stretching his aching legs.

The sun was setting far down Moosehead Lake as John Hanscombe, with Maggie and Grandpa aboard, pulled his one-horse open sleigh up to Mama's cottage in Laketon. Maggie rushed into Mama's arms. "My baby—you're home on Christmas Eve," Mama cried, tears of joy streaming down her face.

❦ ❦ ❦

Late in the afternoon of Christmas Day, the last bit of turkey gone, Mama's plum pudding eaten, the punch bowl nearly dry, "Want to go skating?" Jacky asked.

Jacky and Maggie had received nearly identical pairs of clamp-on ice skates for Christmas. Both wore heavy brown winter shoes with thick horsehide soles from November till April, and these were suited for the steel clamps of their new skates. John had shown them how to screw them into place with the key furnished for each pair.

"Sure. Who's going to be there?" Maggie responded.

"The whole crowd from school. We've got a couple o' acres of ice scraped clear on Moosehead. And a couple of guys helped me lug most of Harry Skillin's old stump fence onto the ice yesterday. Those old cedar stumps'll really light up the night once we get 'em goin' with kerosene an' old rags!"

"Night?"

"Sure. Party starts at nine. We're having a big kettle o' hot chocolate. Two of the girls are bringing popcorn, and when the stumps burn down to coals, we'll shake the poppers until midnight."

Partying until midnight was new to Maggie. Somehow, she decided, she was going to like the idea.

"I've got to meet some guys to finish things up for tonight," Jacky said, rising to pull on his coat. For the first time Maggie noticed how tall he had grown in the year since she had last seen him—and handsome, too! "By the way, my name's Jack," he said decisively, but he smiled as he said it. "See ya 'bout a quarter to nine."

Maggie lay long awake that night thinking. Jacky—Jack—wasn't so bad, after all, she decided. The rude boy had become a polite, considerate young man, nearly as tall as John. John—that was another thing. Jack called him Pa. Once she'd called him Papa, and he actually seemed to like it.

But Jack. Maggie rolled over in bed. He had become friendly and an organizer whom others liked to follow. He'd walked her on his arm to the ice-skating party and even helped her clamp her skates on. Then he'd had little to do with her the rest of the evening, except to ask her to trot back to the house for more milk and chocolate! When he wasn't organizing a game of "snap the whip" or sending others on errands, he was flying around the ice with pretty, blonde Priscilla Perkins.

Pris was a nice enough girl, Maggie knew. They'd had seats across the aisle in the fifth grade. Maggie had helped Pris, who couldn't understand maps or geography with her longitudes and latitudes. They had been rather good friends.

In a few days, Maggie reflected, she'd be heading back to The Elms with Grandpa. He needed her for the rest of the winter, at least. So why worry about Jack and Pris?

Chapter 18

A Funeral at The Elms

It had snowed early that morning on the first day of January 1877, a light snow that gave the spruces, hemlocks, and firs a beautiful frosting, Maggie observed. "We're walkin' in a winter wonderland," Maggie remarked, as she and Grandpa hiked back to The Elms after their Christmas stay with Mama's family at Laketon. "I wish it could stay like this forever."

"Not likely, even for today," Grandpa answered. He wet a finger and held it up to the air. "South wind," he said. "Thaw's comin'. Temperature'll barely dip to thirty tonight. Tomorrow it'll be in the forties."

By noon, the snow had melted. Maggie and Grandpa had both unbuttoned their coats and pulled off their mittens and scarves. They could not find a dry spot to sit, so they ate the sandwiches they had packed for lunch as they walked.

By two o'clock they had reached the forested terrain that sloped downhill toward Allagash Lake. "We'll be home in half an hour—time enough for Jake an' Terence t' get themselves on home before dark," he remarked.

Maggie's ears soon picked up the baying of a running dog far ahead. "Bowser's on the trail of a rabbit," said Grandpa, who had heard it also. "Terence must've given him his freedom. Lucky he didn't show up in Laketon 'bout the day after Christmas."

Maggie smiled, for Bowser was a one-woman dog. Maggie was his mistress, and, like Mary's famous lamb, he followed her wherever she went.

The barking ceased. The two travelers climbed a knoll, then the trail pitched downhill again. Suddenly, from around a bend, shot a long-legged hound, ears flapping, tail high as he ran. Bowser bounded into Maggie's arms and began to lick her cheeks as she knelt on the muddy trail. "Did you miss me, boy?" Maggie cried, scratching behind his ears. "Did you miss your mama?"

For the rest of the journey Bowser happily trotted at Maggie's side, or raced ahead and looped back, as she and Grandpa trudged steadily toward The Elms.

A bridge of two hemlock logs rolled together crossed a narrow brook which ran into the cove where Maggie and Marie had seen the ducks. "Open water," Grandpa noted as they crossed the rapid brook. "And in this stand of hemlocks I'll bet there's a coon tree or two nearby."

"Grandpa, is *that* a coon tree?" asked Maggie, who had given attentive ears to Grandpa's knowledge of the woods. She pointed to a great old hemlock, dead except for several green branches on one side. Its top was broken off, and it appeared to be hollow.

"Could be, sure enough," observed Grandpa. "Perhaps we could investigate tomorrow night, if the moon is out."

"Don't coons hibernate all winter, like bears, unless somebody cuts their tree, like they did over at Eagle Lake Camp?" asked Maggie.

"Some folks think so, but then not everybody's a coon hunter. The coons 'round here likely went to bed in early December, soon's the lakes an' rivers froze up. But come the January thaw, they come out at night to hunt an' fish. Take that hollow back there, full of big ol' hemlocks, with a brook through it. If it stays above freezin' for a day an' a night, the coons wake up an' go fishin' wherever they can find open water."

🐾 🐾 🐾

Grandpa was right about the thaw. The moon rose at eight and the thermometer stood at forty degrees the next evening, when they were ready to hunt coons.

Since Maggie had been with Bowser and Grandpa on several coon-hunting excursions the fall before, he decided it was time she learn to shoot. He got out a .410-gauge, small-bore shotgun for Maggie, and she spent much of the afternoon firing buckshot at a target nailed to the big yellow birch by the lake.

"Stay," Maggie called to Bowser every time she raised her gun to shoot. Though Bowser had been little more than a pup when Maggie had come to The Elms, he had grown into a fine, obedient hunting dog. "I wouldn't trade that hound o' yours for a kennel full of pedigreed huntin' dogs," Grandpa had said on several occasions. "Yes, sir, he's the best!"

Bowser obediently waited for his mistress to fire, then raced ahead of her to the tree to see where she'd hit the target.

"Remember," Grandpa warned, as they carried their guns toward the hemlock hollow in the moonlight, "*don't* cock your gun until you're ready t' shoot, an' don't shoot unless you're sure of your target!"

"I won't," Maggie promised solemnly.

The first shot of the evening was Maggie's. A half-grown young coon scurried up a hemlock leaning over the brook with Bowser at its heels. Maggie called Bowser back, and he sat trembling with delight, the scent of game teasing his nostrils. Grandpa held high his old coach lamp. Maggie could see the coon's eyes shining at her around the trunk of the tree in her moment of frozen excitement.

"Fix him in your gunsight," Grandpa whispered.

"Got him."

"Now pull the gun into your shoulder an' slowly squeeze the trigger."

Maggie squeezed. The gun roared with a nerve-shattering explosion; its tongue of flame seemed to leap at her target in the darkness.

"Fetch him," Grandpa called, and Bowser dived after the fallen coon and placed it at his mistress' feet.

Maggie felt pleasure at having hit the coon on her first try and sickness at having killed a wild animal—she wasn't sure which feeling gripped her the strongest. Her body had goose bumps all over as, lifting the beast by its furry tail, she carried her prize along in the moonlit night.

Suddenly Bowser yelped and raced up the trail, reaching the log bridge ahead of Grandpa and Maggie. The hound leaped from the bridge after his prey. Then coon and dog shot up the brook's bank on the other side into a thicket of firs and hemlocks.

Maggie left her coon on the bridge and laid her gun across it so she could carry the heavy lamp for Grandpa. After plunging through switching evergreen branches and getting struck in the face at least a dozen times, they came into a small clearing dominated by a large, gnarled old black spruce that had blown over. Its top had lodged high in an elm, its huge trunk raised at an angle to the ground.

"Hist!" said Grandpa, pointing to the thickest branches near the tree's top. "Critter's in there—hear it?"

Maggie heard only a rustle, which she thought might be the breeze blowing in the boughs. "Where's Bowser?" she asked.

"Fool dog's followed his nose. Coon's circled back and climbed the tree," Grandpa whispered hoarsely. "He's done that on me before. Now, put some light on that tree, if it'll shine that far."

Maggie raised the heavy brass lamp with both hands, and both she and Grandpa saw a pair of close-set eyes among the limbs at the same time.

Grandpa fired. A black body dropped from the tree.

A second pair of eyes appeared. Grandpa fired the second barrel. Another body fell, this one of a lighter color than the first. Maggie thought it strange that Bowser did not come running at the sound of the gun, but she fought her fears as she followed Grandpa for a look.

Maggie found the coon first, stumbling over it in the dark as she held the lamp up to illuminate the light-colored animal a little further on. She picked herself up, took three more steps, then collapsed on the body of her precious pet. Bowser was dead, shot through the chest with buckshot.

❧ ❧ ❧

Maggie lined Bowser's grave with a thick padding of prince's pine gathered from the shady forest floor that morning. She also gently covered his lifeless body with more pine, then she stood back as Grandpa filled the hole under the comforting, spreading branches of the magnificent, gnarled yellow birch.

As soon as the hole was filled and the sod replaced, Maggie took Grandpa's hammer and a woodworking chisel and engraved this inscription deep into the tree's bark:

Bowser the Hound
March 1875–January 1877

"They don't have funerals for dogs, do they Grandpa?" Maggie asked, as grandfather and granddaughter sat by the sitting room fire half an hour later.

"No, Maggie darling, they don't."

"They don't," Maggie agreed. "Do dogs go to heaven?" Maggie asked, dabbing her tears with a handkerchief.

Grandpa quietly answered, "I don't know, honey."

Maggie was thoughtful. "I'm glad that we *do* know that when people die, if they love Jesus, they go to be with Him. And we'll get to see them again—someday."

"Like your daddy and your Grandma Fuller," Grandpa said gently.

"Yes." Maggie began to cry softly.

Grandpa stepped to her side and patted her head, then kissed her cheek. "Honey, if words can say it, I'm sorry I shot your dog. I had no business firing my gun without knowin' what I was shootin' at. My eyes ain't what they used t' be."

"I know it was an accident, Grandpa." Maggie looked into his sad eyes. "You loved Bowser as much as I did, I think."

Grandpa placed his hand on Maggie's head and sang softly:

> What a Friend we have in Jesus,
> All our sins and griefs to bear!
> What a privilege to carry
> Everything to God in prayer.
>
> Can we find a friend so faithful
> Who will all our sorrows share?
> Jesus knows our every weakness,
> Take it to the Lord in prayer.

Chapter 19

Grandpa Takes a Trip

"Grandpa, I've been thinking," Maggie said at breakfast one morning a few days after they had buried Bowser. "I'm growing up, and I think I want to go home."

"You certainly are growing up," he agreed, noting how well an old hand-knit wool sweater that had once been Grandma Fuller's fit her. She had found it in a bureau drawer, and when she discovered that the sleeves were just the right length, she asked Grandpa's permission to wear it.

"With Bowser gone, I don't feel like a kid anymore. And I'm about done with my grammar schoolbooks— I'm nearly through *McGuffey's Sixth Reader*—so I'll need to go to high school this fall, won't I? And that means Laketon Academy."

"I know it does, honey." After a pause he added, "I may need to make some changes myself. With the loggin' camps movin' north, the company will likely close The Elms, an' I'll be out of work. I'm an old man, though I've been slow to admit it. When your grandma and I were first married, we lived in town for several years. Perhaps I'd better find a place in town an' settle down."

"With that lady from Quebec—the one who writes you?" Maggie giggled.

"Hey, aren't you jumpin' t' conclusions? We're friends—who said anything about marriage?"

Maggie changed the subject, but that afternoon when the company courier brought the mail, he delivered a letter addressed to *Guillaume* Fuller in a delicate female hand. It was from Jeanne d' Arc Lalibertie, Rue de Frontenac, Quebec City, Canada. Grandpa had received a number of such letters, Maggie knew. They had been more frequent since he had traveled to Millinocket in May to buy squash and pumpkin seeds, "on business."

Maggie put Grandpa's letter on a stack she kept next to his reading glasses on the shelf behind the kitchen range. *Guillaume*, she knew, was French for "William." But the letters were written in English, apparently, for Grandpa read them without difficulty. He did have a French-English dictionary that he used when composing letters to *Madame* Lalibertie, sometimes asking Maggie to look up words for him.

Grandpa had another difficulty, though, Maggie realized with concern as she noticed his ivory-framed magnifying glass on the shelf by his glasses. More and more Grandpa resorted to the magnifying glass to read, and she had noticed that one of his blue eyes looked rather cloudy. Too, he seldom read or wrote under the kerosene lamp during these long winter evenings, preferring instead to sit at the kitchen table in a chair in the bright sun by the window each afternoon for an hour or two after lunch, reading or writing with the aid of his magnifying glass while Maggie washed the dishes. Though this often required him to work in the horse barn under lantern light late in the evening, he observed that, "It weren't no use t' try t' read after the sun goes down." *Was Grandpa going blind?* Maggie worried.

A week after Maggie's coon hunt she arose one morning to find the thermometer at twenty-four degrees below zero. The wind had changed, and a cold front had moved in from the west. Within twenty-four hours, the thin layer of water which had formed on the lake ice during the January thaw had frozen solid. "Let's go skatin'," chortled Grandpa. He'd just read another letter from *Madame* Lalibertie, and he was feeling in high spirits. "I've got a couple hours work in the barn yet, shoveling out around them horses. But it can wait till after supper."

"Grandpa, do you *still* skate?" Maggie asked in surprise. She had seen a large pair of clamp-on skates much like her own hanging on a nail above Grandpa's workbench in the shed, but it hadn't occurred to her that he might actually use them. After all, Grandpa hadn't so much as put on his skates during her two winters at The Elms, Maggie knew.

"Sure," he answered jovially. "They say you can't teach an old dog new tricks. But the other side o' that one is that the old dog never forgets the tricks he learned as a puppy. It's been a while, an' I might've lost m' skate key, so I'll have to borrow yours."

In moments, Maggie and Grandpa were laced into their heavy outdoor shoes and trudging across the frozen earth to Allagash Lake. Maggie sat on the boulder and waited for Grandpa to screw the clamps tight with the skate key; then he hitched up onto the boulder and she clamped his on also.

"Let's skate together," Maggie suggested, eyeing the creaky old man walking gingerly across the beach onto the ice. She truly believed he would need her help.

"Later. Just let me skate alone till I get the kinks worked out," he remarked. Grandpa pushed off and sailed like a swan far, far out onto the lake, farther even than Maggie had considered venturing.

Grandpa looped around, then he came sailing back, did a couple of figure eights, reversed directions, and skated backward for a while.

"Now we can try skating together," he said at last, gasping for breath. Maggie took his arm, and Grandpa soon proved to be equally good at skating tandem.

❦ ❦ ❦

"There's no fool like an old fool," Grandpa quoted the next day, as, leaning on his walking stick, he struggled into the kitchen from the barn while Maggie was finishing making breakfast. "I've strained muscles I didn't know I had," he chuckled, though he seemed to be in pain. "Next time I go skatin', I'll try not to behave like a kid."

But "next time" would prove to be another December, when open ice before the heavy snows made for good skating. By the time Maggie and Grandpa had finished breakfast, the air was filled with snow, driven horizontally past the window. The snowfall was so thick that at times it was impossible to see the pump and the old pear tree by the kitchen door.

All night long the storm roared on, as Maggie, snug in her bed, listened to the old house's massive timbers creak and groan in the snow-bearing wind. She remembered God's protection as she lay there, thankful to the Lord for a shed full of firewood and a larder with plenty of meat, potatoes, and vegetables safely stored where they would not freeze. In the morning, however, only a few fluffy clouds were left in the New England sky, though the pump was buried out of sight and the boulder by the lake formed the base of a huge drift extending far onto the ice.

❦ ❦ ❦

March came at last, with its sunny days and windy nights. Grandpa strapped on his snowshoes and traipsed to a row of gnarled rock sugar maples along the back pasture fence, pulling buckets, wooden spouts, a hammer, and a hand drill on Maggie's toboggan. He drilled holes in the trees, pounded in the spouts, and hung a bucket on each one, letting the sweet maple sap drip, glistening in the sun.

Each afternoon for the next two weeks Maggie put on Grandpa's beaver-paw snowshoes, placed a wooden yoke across her shoulders, and with a wooden bucket hung from each end, she tramped back and forth to the trees, bringing the sap to the kitchen. Every inch of the stove was crowded with pans; the sitting room stove was also put to work. The house was filled with steam as Maggie boiled sap into maple syrup for their breakfast pancakes.

During the spring evenings, Maggie played many games of checkers with Grandpa, or she took his dictation as he wrote letters to Jeanne d'Arc Lalibertie. "I've got to plan a trip as soon as the lakes thaw out in April," Grandpa remarked during one of these evening checker games. "An' I've got some decisions t' make."

"About . . . about *Madame* Lalibertie?" Maggie asked hesitantly.

"About Jeanne d' Arc," Grandpa agreed. "We've been writin'—but I've met her only once. We'll take the train to Quebec."

"We? What about the horses?"

"Jake can handle the horses—there's not that many in the barn. Come summer, they're takin' them all up north."

"How do you know *that*?" Maggie knew that for months Grandpa hadn't received any correspondence from company headquarters in Millinocket except his monthly pay, but she didn't want to let on that she'd been studying the envelopes the courier brought them each week.

"Jeanne d' Arc keeps me informed on company business." Maggie thought Grandpa sounded smug when he said it, but she gave him no answer, so he continued. "She was in Millinocket on *company* business last spring, so we decided t' combine business an' pleasure," he continued mysteriously.

"But what's a widow living in Quebec got to do with the business of North Woods Lumber Company? I don't understand!" Maggie protested.

"Ever hear of François Lalibertie?"

"Yes. Oh . . . oh! You mean *the Monsieur* Lalibertie who used to be company president?"

"Exactly. She's his widow. He and she lived at The Elms for more than thirty years and raised their three boys and two girls here. *Madame* Lalibertie was in Millinocket for a company board of directors meeting, since she's part-owner," Grandpa explained, chuckling at Maggie's astonishment.

"Will . . . will you and she live at The Elms. I mean, if you do get married?"

"Oh, no. Jeanne d' Arc has had quite enough of life in the wilderness. She's become quite a city girl."

Maggie got goose bumps thinking of Grandpa's reference to Jeanne d' Arc, whom she guessed must be past seventy, as a "girl." Impulsively she patted his hand. "I understand," Maggie giggled.

He shot her a quizzical look. "Figure I can count on you to come along?" he asked at last.

"Of course. But won't we have to travel to Laketon Junction to catch a train to Quebec?"

"Actually, it's easier to canoe to Cook Camp, then hitch a ride on a log wagon to *Lac* Frontiere, in Quebec, where the Canadian Pacific Railway has a depot. It'll make a nice spring trip."

❦ ❦ ❦

Quebec City is a town of quaint old houses and cobbled streets, narrow and steep, leading up from the northwest bank of the St. Lawrence River, Maggie learned. Grand Gothic cathedrals and old forts, the sites of long-ago battles between the armies of France and England, dotted this walled city. "No city in North America looks more like old Europe," Grandpa related with pleasure as he and Maggie bounced along in a horse-drawn cab from the train depot to *Madame* Lalibertie's house.

"This is Maggie, *non*? How are you, Maggie?" Jeanne d' Arc Lalibertie greeted Maggie at her door. She kissed Maggie on both cheeks, then did the same to Grandpa. Maggie noticed, though, that Grandpa, instead of kissing the woman's lovely old cheeks, bowed and kissed her hand.

Madame Lalibertie was a jovial French lady who spoke English with only a trace of a French accent,

never once asking "how you say it?" *Madame* Lalibertie talked with Maggie as much as with Grandpa,
Maggie noticed. Maggie, in fact, finally found it nec-
essary to excuse herself for a walk along the riverfront
so that Grandpa and Jeanne d' Arc could be alone.

❦ ❦ ❦

"What do you think of Jeanne d' Arc?" Grandpa
asked as the train rolled across the Quebec farmland
toward Maine, after they had spent three days in
Quebec City.

"I think she'd make a very nice grandmother,"
Maggie said decisively.

Grandpa grinned and chuckled. "I agree," was all
he said. But the feeling he put into those two words
told Maggie that he could have said much, much
more.

Maggie found a letter from Mama on the kitchen
table when she and Grandpa returned to The Elms.
Jake had left a long envelope from company headquarters in Millinocket next to it for Grandpa.

> Dear Maggie,
>
>   In May Jack is taking the exams for enter-
> ing the freshman class at Laketon Acad-
> emy. Grandpa reports in his letters that you
> are up to grade level in your studies. So
> why don't you consider taking the exams at
> the same time as Jack?

Grandpa smiled sadly as he read his letter, penned
by a secretary on company stationery. "This is the
official notice," he said. "The Elms is to be closed at the

end of June, and the horses will all be taken to a new stable being built up north. I get a pension starting then."

"Grandpa," said Maggie with a sigh, "it looks as though we're turning our corners together, you 'n' me."

Grandpa grinned slyly. "All the family in Laketon will shortly be invited to a weddin' in Quebec City. I just wish it was closer," he said.

Maggie spent the next morning cleaning her room and packing for the tugboat ride to the railroad terminal at the sawmill the next day. She stopped for a few moments only to scribble a note to Marie and Evangeline LaRochelle, promising a longer one after she got to Laketon. Just before noon Grandpa climbed the shed stairs to Maggie's room and helped her slide her trunk down the steps to the back entry. "You tell your ma if she can't come up here in June, I'll just hire a couple o' men from Eagle Lake Camp to help me pack my belongings for shippin'," he remarked.

"We'll be back—both of us, I promise," Maggie told him. "We can help you pack, even if we can't make the wedding."

After lunch Maggie sat long on the big boulder by Allagash Lake watching the tug tow a raft of logs toward the outlet stream. Closer up, a nut-brown mallard paddled past the beach with her string of fuzzy ducklings in tow.

Maggie counted the ducklings. "Fourteen," she said aloud in quiet amazement, "just the number of the years of my life. And what corners shall I turn next?"

Even as Maggie spoke, the mallard turned, leading her babies straight toward the middle of the lake, bobbing over the rippling wake churned up by the distant tugboat as it steamed away. *And like those ducklings, how God has harbored me from the rough waves of life until I was ready for them*, Maggie mused.

About the Author

Eric E. Wiggin was born in Albion, Maine in 1939, and he grew up with grandparents who could have been Maggie's contemporaries. Like Maggie's father in the book, one of Wiggin's ancestors is buried at Gettysburg. Two of his great-grandfathers served in the Civil War as Union Army volunteers, in the Maine 19th and 29th.

Wiggin once traveled to the Allagash, where there still stands in a woodland intervale a nineteenth-century lumber company horse farm, his model for The Elms.

Author Wiggin has been a pastor, a schoolteacher, a fish plant worker, and a journalist. He now lives with his wife and youngest son, Bradstreet, in rural Fruitport, Michigan. Wiggin and his wife, Dorothy, have a daughter, three sons, and five grandchildren.

Maggie's Homecoming

The Exciting Sequel to
Maggie: Life at the Elms

by Eric Wiggin

After two years in the deep woods with Grandpa, Maggie eagerly returns home. A return to town means returning to school—a scary prospect after two years of schooling herself in the woods. Will she be able to make the grade? And will she and Jack be able to get along with each other? Before Maggie has a chance to settle down, she is caught in a new adventure. One Saturday she and Jack decide to explore a long-abandoned farmhouse around the mountainside from their home—only to find out the place isn't abandoned after all. . . .

Don't Miss Any of the
Addie McCormick Adventures!
by Leanne Lucas

The Stranger in the Attic

A vanishing visitor and secrets from the past . . . Can Addie and Nick put the puzzle together before something terrible happens to their friend Miss T.?

The Mystery of the Missing Scrapbook

A missing scrapbook, mysterious paintings, and an old letter lead Nick, Addie, and Brian on a heartstopping chase. Are they in over their heads this time?

The Stolen Statue

A movie star has been kidnapped and Miss T.'s statue has disappeared! Addie has all the clues . . . but can she put them together before it's too late?

The Chicago Surprise

When Addie and Nick catch a thief, what they discover about the culprit is much more than they bargained for!

The Mystery of the Skeleton Key

In Addie's family history, there's a "treasure" that no one can find! Will Addie be able to solve a mystery that's more than 100 years old?

The Computer Pirate

Someone is stealing information from the school's computer system! Addie's friend is the #1 suspect. Can she prove his innocence?

The Action Never Stops in
The Crista Chronicles
by Mark Littleton

Secrets of Moonlight Mountain

When an unexpected blizzard traps Crista on Moonlight Mountain with a young couple in need of a doctor, Crista must brave the storm and the dark to get her physician father. Will she make it in time?

Winter Thunder

A sudden change in Crista's new friend, Jeff, and the odd circumstances surrounding Mrs. Oldham's broken windows all point to Jeff as the culprit in the recent cabin break-ins. What is Jeff trying to hide? Will Crista be able to prove his innocence?

Robbers on Rock Road

When the clues fall into place regarding the true identity of the cabin-wreckers, Crista and her friends find themselves facing terrible danger! Can they stop the robbers on Rock Road before someone gets hurt?

Escape of the Grizzly

A grizzly is on the loose on Moonlight Mountain! Who will find the bear first—the sheriff's posse or the circus workers? Crista knows there isn't much time . . . the bear has to be found quickly. But where, and how? Doing some fast thinking, Crista comes up with a plan. . . .